T0209699

What We Keep

AND OTHER STORIES

KATHI GARDNER

BALBOA.PRESS
A DIVISION OF HAY HOUSE

Copyright © 2023 Kathi Gardner.

All rights reserved. No part of this book may be used or reproduced by any means, graphic, electronic, or mechanical, including photocopying, recording, taping or by any information storage retrieval system without the written permission of the author except in the case of brief quotations embodied in critical articles and reviews.

Balboa Press books may be ordered through booksellers or by contacting:

Balboa Press
A Division of Hay House
1663 Liberty Drive
Bloomington, IN 47403
www.balboapress.com
844-682-1282

Because of the dynamic nature of the Internet, any web addresses or links contained in this book may have changed since publication and may no longer be valid. The views expressed in this work are solely those of the author and do not necessarily reflect the views of the publisher, and the publisher hereby disclaims any responsibility for them.

The author of this book does not dispense medical advice or prescribe the use of any technique as a form of treatment for physical, emotional, or medical problems without the advice of a physician, either directly or indirectly. The intent of the author is only to offer information of a general nature to help you in your quest for emotional and spiritual well-being. In the event you use any of the information in this book for yourself, which is your constitutional right, the author and the publisher assume no responsibility for your actions.

Any people depicted in stock imagery provided by Getty Images are models, and such images are being used for illustrative purposes only. Certain stock imagery © Getty Images.

Print information available on the last page.

ISBN: 979-8-7652-4331-2 (sc)
ISBN: 979-8-7652-4333-6 (hc)
ISBN: 979-8-7652-4332-9 (e)

Library of Congress Control Number: 2023911566

Balboa Press rev. date: 07/06/2023

To HV, for all you gave to me, especially the one last, best gift.
With deepest gratitude.

Contents

What We Keep

A LONE CANADIAN GOOSE WADES THROUGH THE LATE FEBRUARY SNOW in the park across the street. He raises his head every few steps, stretching his neck and opening his beak, sounding a message. After a few seconds, apparently hearing no response, he plods on. Social creatures, they are seldom far from their flock, and I wonder why this particular goose is alone, here in late winter.

There is a commotion somewhere outside this room and I turn from the window, listening for a moment, but the voices continue down the hall, and when I turn back, the goose is gone, the oddly straight line of footprints stopping at a barely-noticeable disturbance in the snow.

Behind me, the machines keep up a steady cadence, beeps and hisses, at first annoying, now vaguely irritating when I become aware of the sound, which is seldom. She is too silent in the bed, her skin sallow, face sagging away from the bones. To me, she is still beautiful, but that is because we see the ones we love always in their best moments - laughing with delight at something we've said, eyes bright with anticipation when we first meet, face flushed and shining after making love.

Funny how death is the thing we tend to fear the most. We threaten those we hate with killing, we try not to think about our own mortality, shy away from all things connected, and here's the irony - sometimes you don't even know it's happened till it's over.

What I noticed first was that things look a little, well . . . 'off'. There's a subtle change of light, a softening, the colors of things muted, even the sky a shade less blue. You might become aware of your lack of breath, a gradual feeling of stillness, a gentle separation, freedom. Then, slowly, the realization that you no longer need air and that there are other colors, luminescent, not colors you can identify from the spectrum we're familiar with. They seem to emanate from living things, birds, squirrels, rabbits, and of course people. There are so many things to see, to understand, that fear recedes into the background somewhere. After all, the Worst Thing That Could Possibly Happen to you just did, and it's over.

I'd meant to tell you that part of the story later, but it's confusing, because the beginning of this story is the end, as well. So, here is what I'm going to do; I'll go back, and you can follow me back to this room, to the window, and the goose, and the woman in the bed who holds my heart.

Here is the first thing I remember in this life.

I am being carried against my father's shoulder, my head cradled in the cup of his hand as we move from the cool shadows of the living room out through the white French doors at the back of the house and across the sun-dappled lawn. From what Nana Rue tells me later, I am less than three weeks old, yet somehow I know that the light is 'sun,' the movement that ruffles my hair 'breeze,' the sounds from the patio 'speech.'

"Look, there he is," someone says, and other voices –

"He looks like you, Will"

"He's darling. Hello, little man!"

I find myself listening for one particular voice – I do not know why then, only that it is what I need to hear, but I am passed from one pair of hands to another and the voice does not come. Finally, in frustration, I begin to wail.

"Oh, for Lord's sake," someone says, a low, smoky sound, "Give the boy to me."

I am passed along once more, this time into hands that instantly soothe me. There is a calm, a patient knowing in these hands, and I look up, through my tears into a pair of wide grey eyes.

"Hello, Matthew," says my grandmother Ruth Sutton. *She knows me,* I think, and even though her voice is not the one I crave, I turn my face into the safety of her breast and fall instantly asleep.

Nana Ru always cautioned me not to keep jumping ahead.

"You'll get to the end of your life soon enough, Matty," she often told me. I wondered then if that would necessarily be a bad thing, but when I found my life, my real life, I came to understand what she meant.

My name in this life is Matthew Dunway My parents are William, 'Will' and Sheila, my sisters Thalia and Ruth after Nana Ru, my mother's mother.

Growing up, Nana Ru was the person I loved best in the world. My father's people came from Ohio, a beer drinking, groin scratching lot who still call my father 'Billy," and who were convinced that my affection for Nana Ru was a sure sign that I was gay.

My father knew enough to ignore them. He had escaped the clan by getting a scholarship, becoming a data systems analyst, and moving to Santa Rosa, California where he met my mother at the company he worked for. With the help of Nana Ru they bought a huge old house that was in foreclosure and settled in to have children. We all arrived pretty much on schedule, and with parents who loved me and sisters who, when they weren't squabbling, spoiled me rotten, I guess you could say I had an idyllic life as a kid.

Except, of course, for the dreams.

If I had them earlier I can't remember, but my mother said that from the time I was somewhere around two I would awaken sobbing now and then, saying things that were out of sync, asking for the "red truck," mumbling that there was "too much snow" and calling for Mama. Once when I did that she murmured soothingly "Mama's here, Matty," and, barely awake, I responded angrily, "not you, my *other* Mama." Odd, yes, but after raising Thalia and Ruth, she was less disturbed than a new mother might have been. At age three, Thalia went through a period of insisting that she was a raccoon and keeping a bowl of water on the table to 'wash' her food in. Ruth, also creative, saw the Sound of Music at age five, and spent several months afterward wearing a bath towel over her head and explaining that when she grew up she was going to marry Jesus.

There was more than a little of my Nana Ru in my mother, and she accepted her children's peculiarities with little difficulty. Still, it was Nana I confided in when I grew old enough to know that my dreams were not like my siblings' fantasies, not exactly normal.

The first ones I can recall with any clarity were simply random images, faces, fragments of conversation, sometimes a few seconds' view of a place that seemed familiar, but then I would always jolt awake, heart pounding. Since I never knew exactly when they were going to happen, the only control I had was to teach myself to stay calm when I awoke, take deep breaths and try to remember what I had just dreamed. Gradually I developed a system, and by the time I was nine, I kept a small notebook in the drawer next to my bed at home and would write down what

I could recall. I began to pretend that I was a detective trying to work on an important case. It worked great for a while, until the summer I went to stay with Nana Ru while my parents took my two sisters to a cousin's wedding in Ohio.

Ru's home was a brick 1920's bungalow that, when new, was bordered by orange groves to the west and south. As the years passed, developers gobbled up the groves, building closer and closer and offering ridiculous sums of money for the property, first to Grandad Pete, then to Nana after Grandpa succumbed to a heart attack. The more they offered, the less likely it became that Ru would ever sell, as much to thwart the potential buyers, I think, as to stay in the home she loved. At age seventy-four, she gave in to the pleas of a particularly persistent real estate agent. When he arrived, she had opened the attic window and shinnied out onto the roof with a hammer, "looking for loose shingles," as she shouted down to him. She also informed him that she intended to live to be a hundred, and when she finally passed the property would be bequeathed to the nearby Buddhist monastery as housing for guests. Not true, of course, but Ru had a penchant for embellishment of the facts, especially with people she had little use for.

I loved staying with Ru. The attic was full of boxes of cool stuff which Ru let me rummage through unchecked. She also let me pick dinner, usually pizza or hot dogs, and talked to me as if I were a real grown person, not a child. I slept in my Uncle Tony's old room across the hall from hers, and we stayed up late if there was a baseball game - it didn't matter what team - on TV. Ru would curse her least favorite team in markedly creative ways, stopping at some point to roll her eyes at me.

"Matthew, don't ever let your mother catch you using that sort of language," she'd say sternly. "It's a wretched habit, right up there with cigarettes and drinking grain alcohol. I can't unlearn it now, I'm too old, but *you* know better. Don't start."

There was almost a full moon that night, and the light made a path across the floor at the foot of Uncle Tony's bed. I drifted off to sleep easily, but at some point the dream began. This time I was angry at somebody, a boy, I think, yelling at him. I could see his face, white, ashamed. "But Dad," he was saying and I was furious, turning away from him.

"I don't want to hear your lame excuses," I said, and then that voice, hers. "Don't be so hard on him, my love," she said, and I snapped awake, sweating, a moan lodged in my throat. Ru was standing in the moonlight path by the bed, her hand soft on my forehead.

"Nightmare, Matty?" she asked softly.

I shook my head. I had become adept at secrecy by then, but something made me want to tell Ru that night what was happening to me.

"Not nightmares," I said hesitantly. "Just dreams about things, people."

"Things that scare you, like monsters?"

"No," I said, not monsters. *Real* things, places, people, but not from now."

I sat up, grabbing my pillow and squashing it in frustration. "It's like I'm remembering something, only I can't get it all, like when you click the TV remote really fast and just see a little bit of a show, but when you try to go back, you can't find it. I want to see more, but I can't - I always wake up."

"I see," Ru's voice was an anchor in the dark, calming me. "Do you think perhaps you might have seen these people before?"

"I dunno," I said, sighing. "Maybe, I guess - but how could I? The one tonight called me Dad. I'm not old enough to be a dad!

And sometimes there's a lady, I hear her voice and it makes me feel really weird - happy and sad, and warm and-"

To my horror, I began to cry.

Ru reached for me, moving away the pillow and pulling me against her shoulder. She said nothing till I regained my composure, wiping my nose on my pajama sleeve.

"Come on, let's go to the kitchen."

I climbed onto one of the tall chairs at the breakfast bar and settled myself while Ru gathered the ingredients for a milkshake out of the fridge, whirred it all in the blender, then set a tall glass in front of me and a small one for herself, another of the forbidden pleasures we secretly enjoyed.

"Matty," she said once we had both taken a satisfying drag on our straws. "I'm not going to lie to you. I don't know what is going on in your dreams any more than you do. Maybe as you get older, they'll go away. Odd things happen in the world, things that we can't explain. The first moment I saw your grandfather, halfway across a convention hall full of people, I knew that I *knew* him, and that I would love him for the rest of my life, and I never questioned it. I think when we question things too much we begin to doubt the reality of them and perhaps they stop happening, or perhaps we stop ourselves from letting them happen. Do you understand what I mean?"

"I think so, Nana," I said.

"Maybe what you have, Matty, is a gift. Don't be afraid of of it," Ru said. pouring the last dab of milkshake into my glass, "but if you ever do feel afraid, come and tell me and we'll see what we can do to fix it, OK?"

I nodded, a soft blanket of drowsiness draping itself over me. Ru stood, came to put her arm around my shoulders.

"C'mon," she said, easing me off the kitchen stool. "Let's get you back to bed, I'll sit with you for a while till you get back to sleep."

As usual, Ru gave me the sense that everything was all right.

The dreams continued to ebb and flow with no discernable pattern. Sometimes weeks would go by undisturbed, then one or two fragments would surface in as many days. Bolstered by Ru's unwaveringly calm response, I kept making notes, learned to recognize faces, (although I had no names to match.) I even became aware of settings; snow, an unlikely image for a born-and-raised California boy to conceive of, was present in a number of the dreams, as well as bare trees, rolling green pastureland, and gravel roads.

I learned to trust Ru with other things as well. When my friends began to notice girls, I wondered if something was wrong with me. I liked them, of course, thought some of them were pretty, smart, but none of them drew me in the way that I assumed that they were supposed to. My mother noticed before anyone else, and asked me what felt like intensely personal, probing questions, but it was Ru I turned to.

"Mom thinks there's something wrong with me," I told Ru. "I think she thinks I might be gay."

"Do you think so?"

"No. I just don't - I don't know, it's just that the girls in my school seem so, I don't know, so immature. And —" I hesitated.

Ru waited me out.

"It's just that there's really nobody I've met that I want to date. I like girls, but they're just girls."

"You're fine, Matty," Ru said calmly. "Eventually you'll meet someone, but in the meantime you need to get some practice. Go on a few dates, have fun with your friends. It will make your mother happy, and she'll find something else to obsess about."

Ru grinned. "What about Holly, your friend from the yearbook staff?"

I shrugged, I liked Holly, and I knew she had a crush on me. "I guess," I said. "She's pretty cool. We talk a lot, and I don't get bored."

"There you are, then," Ru said, sounding as though the matter was settled.

It was, more or less. We dated until the end of our senior year in high school, did the usual experimenting with sex that happens at that age, and parted amicably after graduation, headed for different schools. In retrospect, Holly knew me better than I knew myself, and she knew when it was time to move on, but in this one thing, Nana Ru was mistaken. No one came along who could settle into the empty space I carried inside myself.

Music filled the space for a time, or at least made it feel smaller. By the time I graduated from high school, I thought music was what I wanted to study. My Dad muttered under his breath at the probable inability of my making any substantial living "noodling around" with it, even though I had a talent for the guitar that had landed me several paying gigs in local coffee houses during the summer months. He finally, grudgingly agreed to let me study music at UC Santa Barbara, as long as I "backed it up with something solid like I did, son."

College was different, better. I felt as though at last I fit in somewhere, and although I dreamed, my waking life seemed to finally be more important, or at least *as* important, as the bits and pieces of that other life half remembered. There were girls, some drinking, friends, and I found that computers didn't bore me as much as I'd thought they might, plus I had some of my father's talent, so I made it through with what seemed like minimal effort.

It was at my graduation party that I saw how frail Ru had become. Her silver hair was white, thinning, her walk tentative.

True, I had seen her at holidays, but with the usual crowd at our house and all the excitement, Thalia's new baby, Ruth's penchant for drama, I'd somehow missed her gentle decline, and it scared me.

"Nana," I said, putting an arm around her shoulders, "I've got a job, did Dad tell you? In Minnesota, with a firm that services library systems."

"Good for you, Matthew," she said, her voice softer than I recalled. "When do you leave?"

"In two weeks," I told her. "Can I come see you before I go?"

"Of course, love," she nodded. "You'll have to stay on the couch downstairs, though. I've closed off all the bedrooms upstairs, too much work for me to get up there now. Your mother wants me to move into a senior center, but you know I can't do that, too damn stubborn."

When I arrived at the house a few days later, I realized the toll four years had taken. The flowerbeds on either side of the porch were overgrown, the lawn patchy, and inside the woodwork no longer shone with lemon oil, the rugs shabby, blinds with a fine film of dust.

As usual, we talked of everything. The time flew by the first day, and I was Matty again, Ru was the same irrepressible, outspoken, loving presence who was my touchstone. Late that night, though, things changed. We were sitting on opposite ends of the old, rumpsprung couch where I'd sleep that night, when Ru reached over and touched my knee.

"How are you, really, Matty?" she asked. "Still dreaming?"

I nodded. "Not as bad now," I told her. "When it happens, it's more like I'm just remembering something from a movie I saw or a book I've read. I'm so used to it that it doesn't upset me like it used to."

Ru nodded. "But it still happens now and then?"

She sat quiet for a moment, staring off into space, then took my hand. "Matty, I want to tell you something, so please just listen. All my life I've had these flashes of intuition, deja vu or whatever the Hell you want to call them. They scared me, too, at first, but I didn't tell anyone. Your great gran, my mother, was so religious I was afraid she'd think I was possessed. Over time, I came to believe that they were simply leftover memories we keep from another life. I didn't tell you when you were younger because I didn't want to scare you worse than you already were, but I'm telling you now because I won't be here too much longer."

"Don't say that," I blurted.

"Shhh, hon. It's true. Peter promised he'd come for me when it was time, and it's going to be soon, but I'm fine with it. I'm tired, Matty, and there isn't anything left for me to do that I want to do. What I do want, my dear, is for you to be happy, truly happy, whatever that takes."

'I'll try," I told her. "I just don't know what that is right now. I'm happy about the job, I guess – I've always wanted to go somewhere different."

Ru smiled. "You'll be ok, Matty, I know you will. Do what you have to do, and don't let anybody tell you not to. It's worked for me all these years."

I'd been at the job for five months and was just getting used to carrying a jacket in the car – April weather in Minnesota varies minute to minute – when Mom called, crying. Like everything else in her life, Ru had followed her own schedule. When she didn't answer Mom's daily phone call, she went over and found envelopes addressed to herself and each of us grandkids, the kitchen tidied up, and Ru in her favorite chair overlooking the backyard, knitting in her lap and a smile on her face meant for grandpa Peter, who must have come as promised sometime the day before.

"I'll come home," I said, but Mom declined. "No, Matt, there isn't going to be a funeral. You know your grandmother -her instructions were crystal clear in my letter. She's to be cremated and her ashes strewn around the base of the old pear tree in the back corner of the yard, 'where Peter is,' she said. Did you know about that?"

I denied it, but of course I did know – Ru had told me how she'd slipped out at night to put his ashes there and refilled the urn that sat on the mantel in the family room with sand and pea gravel from the front flowerbed. That, she said, is where he wanted to be, and it was no business of anyone's but hers and Peter's.

Ru left something to everyone. Thalia, who loved to garden, got the house with strict instructions to take care of the fruit trees; Ru and I each got a very generous amount of money and told to do "something wild and outrageous" with it, which is how I ended up cruising the countryside outside of Minneapolis on my Harley Street 500 in late May.

It was a beautiful day, warm and a little breezy, and I was thinking about Ru, how she would have loved to be behind me on the bike. Strangely, I wasn't sad – I knew Ru was exactly where she wanted to be – but I was lonely. On the weekends I'd taken to riding for a few hours if the weather was good, sometimes meeting a few of the people from work at a bar in the evenings, but none of it seemed to fill the empty space that had always been there inside me.

I slowed down a little to read the hand lettered sign near the drive of an old farmhouse. I'd bought eggs, maple syrup, honey this way, and it was still new to me, seeing what was offered, but this sign was different.

"Help wanted. Selling soon, need small repairs, yard work. Will pay. Ring bell."

I turned in and up the long, curving drive, parking in the gravel yard next to what looked to be the fieldstone foundation of a long-gone barn. The doorbell looked much newer than the sagging screen door, and I rang it, not really expecting an answer as there was no car visible. I was just about to turn away when I heard footsteps and the scarred wooden door was wrenched open.

The woman was an inch or so taller than me, a thick silver braid hanging over one shoulder. Her eyes were hazel, smile lines radiating from the corners, and she held my gaze steadily.

"Yes? Can I help you?"

I don't know how long it was before I answered. All the fleeting images I'd seen, the scraps of conversation I'd heard in my dreams, the longing I sometimes felt on waking coalesced when she spoke, and I instantly knew her voice, her touch.

"I'm here about the sign." I finally said.

"I don't recognize you," she said, slightly puzzled. "You're not one of the neighbors, are you?"

"No. I work in Minneapolis, just out on my bike, but I saw the sign. I can do some stuff, my grandmother taught me a lot about gardening and I'm pretty good with tools." I realized I was babbling.

"So you're just free on weekends?"

"No, I could come evenings, too," I told her. "If that's OK?"

"We'll see," she says. "I'm Grace Britten. And you are?"

"Matthew Dunway."

"Well, Matthew, let me show you what needs to be done. A lot of it is weeding, trimming, making things look good for perspective buyers. I'm not putting it on the market until September, so there's time, and there are a few indoor repairs,

13

some spackling and painting once you're done with the outside work."

We walked the property, larger than it looked from the road and needing a fair amount of work. Grace talked, pointing out what she wanted done, and I just listened. When we got back to the house, Grace stopped, gave me a piercing look.

"Are you up for it?" she asked.

I nodded.

"Then you'd better come in, we can talk money and I'll show you the rest of the place."

The front door opened directly into the kitchen, a long, welcoming room that ran the entire length of the house with French windows that surrounded two sides, a rustic oak table set at one end overlooking the small orchard at the back. An archway to the left led into a small sitting room where a large tabby curled at one end of the gray couch, one eye half open, scoping out my intentions.

"That's Max, the man of the house," Grace told me.

"This room is perfect," I told her, walking further into the kitchen.

She smiled. "I saw a kitchen like this once when I looked at a house with a friend. When I agreed to move with Jim from the city, this was the deal breaker. I made him promise to make me my dream kitchen or I wouldn't come."

"You don't like the country?"

"I grew up in the country, and it's beautiful and peaceful, but for me now, being by myself, it feels a bit isolated. Sit down, please. Would you like some coffee?"

"Yes, thanks, black." I nodded. "I'm from California, and I've always lived in a city, but my gran always said I was born lonely, so I guess country living wouldn't matter to me."

Grace turned from the counter, setting two cups on the table and joining me.

"Someone I once knew used to say that same thing," she said. "So, Matthew, what do you think?"

I would have done it all for nothing, just to see her again, but instead I named a ridiculously low sum, we haggled, and finally settled on a price – and then we talked.

I told Grace about my IT job, and she told me about her former career as a court reporter, moving to the farm, losing her husband Jim over a year ago. It was getting late when I finally left, but only after Grace insisted I get home before dark.

"I'm glad you stopped, Matthew," she said. "That sign has been up for three weeks, and not a bite. You go home safe now, I'll see you on the weekend."

I reached out to shake her hand, and when it slipped into mine, it took everything I had to let it go. For a few seconds, a puzzled look crossed her face, and I wondered if Grace felt it too, but she stepped back, smiling, and closed the door.

We fell quickly into a routine. I would come early Saturday mornings, would work till late afternoon. Grace loved to cook, and would call me in to feed me before I left. I offered to stay and help with dishes every time, so she washed while I dried and we chatted. For Grace, I think, talk didn't come easily, but for me it was like finally coming home from a long trip. I told her about my life, and mostly she listened, fully connected.

Of course we talked about Ru. She laughed over the roof story, and when I mentioned how Ru had smuggled Peter's ashes into the garden and wanted hers there with his, she sighed.

"I was in love with someone like that once," she said. "It was a long time ago. Jim was gone a lot for work, and I didn't mind, really. I was busy with the house, friends, my job, but when I met Hal, it was different, like music."

"Music?"

"You know how sometimes you will hear a piece of music for the first time and it grips you? It settles into your soul so that from then on you can hear just the first two or three notes and you hear the whole song in your mind. It was like that, like music."

"What happened?"

I thought at first she wasn't going to answer.

"Not even the best things last forever, Matt. We both moved on. I had Jim, and Hal needed to be somewhere away from his past, away from here."

She got up from the table, signaling an end to the conversation.

As the days lengthened into summer, I stayed later, wanting to be as near Grace as long as I could.

"There's a spare bedroom upstairs at the end of the hall, Matt," Grace told me one afternoon. "It hasn't been used in years, but if you want you could stay there on weekends so you don't have to make the trip so often."

I threw a few things in my gym bag on a Friday night and headed out, planning an early start Saturday morning. When I arrived, Grace was cooking, as usual.

"Go on up," she told me. "Last door on the right. I dusted, put on fresh bedding, but don't expect much. Haven't been up there in over a year."

It was a small room but bright from two corner windows. I tossed my bag on the floor and turned to go, stopped dead.

Next to the bed was a small mahogany side table with a mirrored top tinted blue.

I knew that table. I stared at it as images came flooding in. I'd grown used to the dreams, but this was completely different, a memory that I couldn't have had yet was there, vivid.

When it finally stopped, I took some deep breaths, shook myself and went slowly back downstairs.

Grace put plates in front of us and settled across the corner from me, and we ate, chatting about my plans for trimming the overgrown ivy around the barn. When we were done, Grace poured the last of the coffee into my cup and was standing at the sink, rinsing the plates.

"So, that table by the bed upstairs. It's really unusual," I said casually. "Where did you find it?"

Grace went still, so still I thought she hadn't heard me. Finally, she turned.

"I bought it years ago at an antique mall. I saw it in a booth, and it was so lovely, I really wanted to buy it, but there was no price. They told me the owner was in the basement, cleaning up, so I went looking for him. There was this man pushing a broom across the floor with his back to me."

"I said, 'There's a blue mirrored table upstairs I'd like to buy. Is it yours?' He told me, "It's cobalt glass-"

"And it's yours now," I finished the sentence for her.

She moved to the table and dropped into a chair, staring at me, her face gone pale.

"That's exactly what Hal said. How could you possibly know?"

"Look, Grace, I know this sounds crazy, but listen, please," I said.

"All my life, since I was a kid, I've had these dreams, usually just fragments of something that seemed like it happened to me, even though it couldn't have. It never made any sense, none of it, but when I saw that table - I think somehow I was there. When you answered the door that first day, I heard your voice and it was like everything came back to me." I trailed off.

"Go on," she said.

I told her all of it, at least everything I could remember that made sense; repeated dreams of a red truck, driving in the snow, bits and pieces of conversation. When I got to the boy calling me Dad, she reached out, laid her hand on my arm.

"Hal's son, Barry, got caught shoplifting at Target once," she said. "Just a foolish teenaged prank, a CD he liked. I was with Hal when he got the call, went with him to the police station to pick Barry up, and he was so angry, furious! I'd never seen him so upset, and I had to get him to sit in the truck to calm down before we went in."

We sat, not speaking, till the kitchen was almost dark. Finally, Grace sighed.

"I don't doubt you, Matt, but I'm stunned. I've been comfortable with you since the moment we met, but this is too much, I don't know how to process what you're telling me. I'm tired, and it's been a long day, I'm going up to bed. We can talk in the morning."

I nodded.

I sat on the back porch for an hour or so, watching the cat stalking something under the hedge, then went up myself.

The mattress was old, sagging but comfortable, and I fell asleep as soon as my head hit the pillow, but not for long.

At first, the sound became part of the dream I was having, but gradually I came awake and it was still there, thunder mumbling through the night, coming closer, rain beginning to patter on the porch roof outside my half-open window. I got up, lowered it a few inches, then went to check the one in the bathroom that I'd left open wide after I showered earlier. Grace's door was ajar, and as I walked past I caught a glimpse of her standing at her window, curtain drawn back, watching the distant lightning.

I couldn't stop myself. I pushed open the door, walked across the room to her. Grace heard me and turned.

"It's you, Grace," I said. "I feel like I've been looking for you all my life."

"Oh, Matt," she whispered, lifting her hand to cradle my cheek. "This makes no sense. I can't."

"Please," I said, turned my face into her palm, put my lips to the inside of her wrist.

Her skin was silk, smelled faintly of lilac, and tasted exactly as I knew it would. I moved closer, pulled her against me, kissing her neck, then her mouth.

Everything that happened then was from memory- her hands in my hair, her head thrown back, moaning, her back arching up to meet me when I moved inside her, both of us desperate, fusing together while the thunder rolled overhead. She called a name out that wasn't mine, but it didn't matter, I knew she was calling for me.

After, I wrapped myself along the curve of her back, skin to skin, my face buried in her hair and fell into the dreamless dark.

It was early when I woke, just turning light, but the smell of coffee wafted up from the kitchen.

I'm not sure what I expected that morning – a kiss, an embrace, some acknowledgement of what was, for me, a life-altering night.

Grace was sitting uncharacteristically silent at the table, staring into the mug she clasped tightly in both hands. I grabbed a cup and joined her, not knowing what, if anything, I should say.

It was Grace who finally broke the silence.

"Last night, Matthew. Last night was a gift, but also a mistake." She looked up at me, and I saw that she'd been weeping.

"I've had so many losses in my life. You are just at the very beginning, but you'll find that every time you lose someone you love, it takes away a piece of you. I'm missing a lot of pieces, my dear, too many, and I'm too old. I can't go through it again."

"But I'm here, Grace," I said, putting my hand on her wrist. "I won't go anywhere. If it's about what people will think –"

"I've never once worried about what people will think of me, and I'm not going to start now. I don't have enough time left."

I shook my head.

'I mean it, Matthew. It's why I'm moving, selling the place. I'm old, this body is just wearing out, and I'm OK with that, but you have a whole, lifetime to fall in love, make mistakes, make memories." She patted my hand and gently moved her arm away.

"You should go finish trimming the lilac bush. It's supposed to rain later."

I spent the rest of the morning outside, going over what I could say to Grace to change her mind, but knowing there was probably nothing. The clouds started to roll in once more around noon, so I went in. Grace was in the living room, Max on her lap, eyes closed,

"Looks like the rain is coming again," I said. "Guess I'll head back to the apartment. It's supposed to set in till tomorrow."

Grace opened her eyes.

"I think that's probably best, Matthew," she told me. "There's a check on the table for you."

When I came downstairs with my bag, she was still sitting there, but as I walked toward the back door she spoke.

"Matthew? Please be careful, OK?"

"OK," I said.

It was still drizzling off and on when I left. Once off the long gravel driveway, I sped up, trying not to think. I don't remember very much of that trip, just that I needed to move fast, feel the wind on my face, the bike motor thrumming under me, blot out the noises in my head.

I never heard the truck.

So here we are. Time moves differently on this side. I know I was in the place where we rest for a while so I'm not sure how long it has

been since that day, but Grace looks older, her skin translucent, hair more white than silver now.

She sensed me a few hours ago, opened her eyes, looked toward the window where I'm standing and smiled a little. She's floating in between there and here right now, but it won't be long before she can see me waiting.

This time, I'll take her hand and won't let go.

Big Sugar

MOST SUMMER EVENINGS, AFTER THE SUN DROPS THE TREE LINE and it cools off some, Mo'ma and I take ourselves out to the front porch to sit awhile, me on the swing and her in the big old creaky wicker rocker. I like to stick my foot out and push against the porch railing to swing myself while Mo'ma rocks. When it's been really hot, the mists start to move up out of the earth like spirits. It used to make me feel spooky when I was small, but Mo'ma says it comforts her, like memories - always there, just rising up now and then to make you look.

I've been coming here to Georgia to be with Mo'ma every summer since I was eight. She's my mama's grandma. Her real name is Maura Robbins, but when I was little I couldn't say Great Grandma Maura, so I called her Mo'ma. It was Mama's idea to send me down that first year. My grandma died before I was born, so Mo'ma is the only real grandma I've got, and I hadn't seen her since I was two, only talked to her on the phone when Mama called her and I happened to be around, so I only knew her from her voice. Mo'ma lives all alone in this old house, and sometimes I think she gets lonely . I guess Mama thought so, too 'cause she just told me it was time to get to know my great -grandma, and that I was going by Mo'ma's for awhile, no arguments. After that first summer, I wanted to come back again real bad, waited for it every year like Christmas.

Mama says Mo'ma and I look alike. Our eyes are almost the same color - hazel, Mama calls it - and when we sit out here on the porch, the dampness teases little wisps of Mo'ma's hair away from the knot in back, no matter how tight she winds it. My hair is all over the place too, darker than hers but the same kind of wild. Mo'ma's hair was red once, but now it's mostly all grey and white.

"Sure an' lookin' after you is what's done it," she tells me, teasing. I have just a few freckles, not as many as Mo'ma, but all the time she spends in the garden has browned her so they don't show so much. I'm glad, I think, to look like her.

Lately, now that I'm older, we don't talk as much as we used to, but tonight I feel like hearing Mo'ma's voice, the music of it. It makes me imagine Ireland, where Mo'ma was born, all green and blue and everybody sounding like her when they talk.

"Tell me a story, Mo'ma," I say. "Tell me about when you met great grampa Sug." It's my favorite story, and even though Mo'ma tells it to me every time I come to visit, I never get tired of hearing it.

Mo'ma settles down into her chair and begins to rock slow and even.

"Fifteen, I was," she says, " standin' in front of Early's Dry Goods Store on Carroll Street, lookin' at a bolt of paisley goods for a spring dress. The wind was whippin' about like always in Chicago, my hair every which-a-ways and me tryin' to hold it down with one hand and my purse in t'other, when this voice says to me "What that fine hair needs is a good braidin'." So, I turn around and there's this big man, broad as a barn, hands on his hips just grinnin' away.

"And what would you be knowin' about braidin hair, just tell me that!" I says to 'im."

"Well," he says, " When I was a boy I'd see my Mama braid her own hair and my sisters' 'most every day, that's what. I guess I'd know somethin' about it."

Mo'ma sighs, and her face goes all soft. "Man had the voice of an angel, so deep it made me think of the way the earth smells when you turn it in spring for the garden, all rich and sweet. Made me so I couldn't move, standin' in front of the Dry Goods like an ijut with me hair a mess, an' him just lookin' at me and smilin'."

"Well," Mo'ma says, shifting a little in her chair to get comfortable, "it didn't take long for himself to find out that I worked in the laundry two blocks over. I went in four in the mornin' to noon then, unless they needed me extra, and don't I come out the back door into the alley on the next Tuesday to find himself standin' there smug as you please with a big bunch of flowers in his hand. Daisies, they were, in April! Lord knows where he got 'em."

"Ma'am," he says, handin' them over to me. I like to die! I looked around to see if anyone was about, an then I lit into him. "What the divil are ya' thinkin," I says, "comin' after me at the place I work, bringin' me flowers like you're courtin'. Are ya daft, then?"

Now, a regular man woulda been done right then, gone off and never looked back," Mo'ma says, "but not your great grandfa'ar. He just looks at me steady with them big eyes of his an' says "Yes, ma'am - and no, ma'am."

"What's THAT supposed to mean?" I ask 'im."

"Yes, ma'am, I reckon' I am courtin', an no, ma'am, I'm not crazy, if that's what you mean," he says.

Mo'ma reaches over to the little table between us and takes up her tumbler of lemonade. The glass is all foggy on the outside, and the ice is almost gone. She takes a little sip, holds the glass to her cheek to catch the coolness.

Now usually comes the part I like best, the part about how great grampa and Mo'ma came to this house to live, but tonight something is different. Mo'ma looks at me, a long look, measuring. Then she settles back in her chair and her voice gets low, serious.

"Seems as though I spent all my time watching to see if there was anyone seein' us," Mo'ma says. "Your great granfa'ar Sug was a strong man, bless him - he knew what he wanted, an' he held fast to get it. Came to that alley door every day for three weeks straight. His boss thought well of him, so most times he'd let Sug borrow the delivery van once he got through with his milk route. I'd come out the door and there he'd sit, smilin' that smile and talkin' me up in that way he had, an' all the time me watchin' for fear somebody who knew Pa would catch us."

"Mo'ma, how come great grampa was called Sug?" I say. Mo'ma shoots me a look. She hates to be interrupted.

"Do y' want to hear this story, or not?" she asks, not expecting an answer.

"If y' must know, yer great grandfather always had a sweet tooth, he did. His sister Louella was the same, but Lawrence, he was a big, solid boy, an Louella was just a mite, so their father called them Big Sugar an' Little Sugar, an' it stuck. Now, where was I?"

"Ah, yes. My Pa, your great great grandfather Doolan, was a hard man, awful hard," Mo'ma says. "Brought his whole family here from the old country for things to be better, an' worked himself to the bone to make it so, that much I'll give him, but everythin' had to be his way or none at all. Bad enough I was the second girl and me older sister without so much as a prospect of marriage yet. T'wouldn't be proper for me to be promised 'fore Mary Agnes, let alone to someone who wasn't Catholic," Mo'ma said. "If word had gotten to Pa I was seen consortin' with some strange man in the alley next the laundry, it'd have been the end of me for sure, and him along with me."

Mo'ma trails off, her voice getting lost in the Junebug's buzz and hum. It's getting dark, and the deer that live in the woods beyond Warren's hayfield across the road have come out to graze. I can just see them moving along the edge of the trees, every now and then a flash of white tail switching off the mosquitos. I watch them, stepping high in the tall grass, all awkward like this boy at school I like. His name is David, and he's skinny like a deer, all legs and big brown eyes. I think maybe I'm in love with him, but I haven't told anybody but Mo'ma. I knew she wouldn't fuss, tell me I'm too young, and all that other stuff I don't want to hear.

"We'd get in the milk wagon and Sug would drive us over to the lake," she says. "We'd sit an' watch the water an Sug'd tell me all about his folks, his brothers and sisters, and how he sent money to his parents every payday. He'd talk about how green an' pretty it was where he grew up. Made it sound like Tennessee was Heaven's doorstep, he did. Lord love 'im, the man could spin a tale."

Mo'ma sighs.

"I finally decided I better tell Ma I was seein' someone 'fore somebody found out an' raised Hell," she says. "I told her I was bein' courted, and that he wasn't Church. She nearly flew, she was so upset. I can still recall her wringin' a corner of her apron an' frettin' at me. "It'll be the end of yer father," she says, "the end. You keepin' company with a man without us knowin', and a Protestant, at that. At least I hope he'll have the common decency to come an' ask after yer Pa's permission. Y'know there'll be no weddin' till Mary Agnes is at least spoken for. I don't know what y'were thinkin' of.""

"I set it up with Ma to bring him by on a Sunday, after dinner. Pa was usually in a passing good frame of mind then, an' I figured it'd be then or never at all. Sug showed up prompt at 2:00 o'clock with some flowers for me Ma, an' I was watchin' through the kitchen window for him."

Mo'ma is quiet for a long time. I think maybe she has gone to sleep, but when I look over at her, she is staring out into the dark at something only she can see.

"What happened, Mo'ma?" I ask.

"Ah, child," Mo'ma says, shaking her head. "When Sug came in he walked right up to me Ma and said, "Mrs. Doolan, ma'am, these are for you. I thank y' for letting me come to your home." Ma didn't say nothin', just stood there starin at him like she'd been poleaxed. Mary Agnes was afraid she'd faint, grabbed her firm around the waist an' hushed her like you would a child. See, I told Mary Agnes about Sug right off. We were close then - I knew she'd help me out, if it came to that."

This is a part of the story I never heard before. I want to ask Mo'ma why her Ma was so upset, but I know how Mo'ma gets, so I just shut up and sit real still.

"I go in the parlor where Pa's readin' the paper," Mo'ma says, "an I say 'Pa, this is Lawrence Robbins come to speak to you.' Pa looks up at 'im, an puts the paper down real slow, stands up.

"An' what might you be here for, then?" Pa says.

"Well, sir," Sug says, holdin' out his hand to shake, "I've come to ask after your daughter Maura."

Pa just stands there, lookin' up at Sug, quiet, but I can see the red creepin' up from his collar, gettin' darker by the second. When we were young, I used to fancy Pa got bigger when he got mad, an' I could see it then, him swellin' up, Sug standin' there with his hand out an' Pa ignorin' it. Finally Pa yells "Rose! ROSE

DOOLAN! Get in here!" an' Ma scuttles in from the kitchen, shakin' like anything.

"Look, will ye," Pa roars. "Lookit what yer daughter's gone an' done." Pa's so mad spit's flyin' from the corners of his mouth like a rabid dog, an he comes at me, gets in my face. "Is this a bloody joke, then?" Pa yells. "Have ye gone mad, bringin' some heathen inta our home, bold as y' please?"

I'm mad, now, too, so mad I'm tremblin' meself, but then Sug steps up, puts his shoulder between Pa an' me and takes my hand in his, and his hand is warm, solid, not shakin' at all.

"Sir," Sug says, "I hoped Maura's family -" but Pa cuts him off short. "That girl's got no family in this house," he says.

"Thomas!" me Ma says, but Pa shuts her mouth with a look.

Sug stands lookin' at Pa, and I see right then the man Sug is. I see that Sug's not afraid of Pa, that he'll stand up to'im to protect me.

"Come on Maura," Sug says then. He turns me away from Pa an' we go out through the kitchen, past Mary Agnes cryin', an' down the steps. I can still hear Pa yellin' "The divil take ye both" after us as we're walkin' away."

We sit quiet in the dark, listening to the tree frogs calling each other across the lawn and the steady creak of Mo'ma's chair. Pretty soon the yard light clicks on, and she jumps a little, startled.

"I couldn't help it," Mo'ma says. "Halfway down the block I starts to cry too. "Well, that's done it!" I says to Sug. "I've got no family now." He stops, puts his arm 'round me shoulders right there in the street, an' he says, 'Well, then, Maura, I guess we'll have to make our own."

"Himself took me to a boardin' house, one for proper workin' girls, an' gave me the money to pay the landlady a week's lodgings," she says. "Ma an' Mary Agnes brought me a carpetbag with my clothes in it while Pa was at work. There were laws about us marryin' then, but Sug's friend Earl was a preacher, and he said God's law was the only one that really mattered, so a week later he married us. Mary Agnes wanted to come, but I told her no. No sense making Pa any madder than he already was."

Mo'ma stops rocking then. She is quiet for a long time. Then she gets up, slow, and goes in, lets the screen door bang shut behind her. Mo'ma is always yelling at me not to bang the door, and I get worried, but just as I'm getting up to go see to her, she comes back, flipping on the porch light on her way out. This time, she shuts the door quiet, walks over and hands me a picture.

"Your great grandfa'ar's friend Earl took that picture the day we were wed," she says, sitting down heavy in the rocker. "Said it was only fitting we have a memento of the occasion. Be careful with it, now, 'tis the only one I have."

The picture is small, yellowed and curling around the edges. I smooth it flat against my knee ever so gently and hold it up toward the porch light.

I look hard at the picture. I see now why my hair is so tight and dark, why I don't freckle so bad the way Mo'ma does in the sun - and I guess I see what it is that made Mo'ma's Pa so angry.

The man in the picture is big, not so tall, but solid, broad in the shoulders, and his skin is very, very dark. He is smiling, a wide, sweet smile, and Mo'ma's small white hands are folded gently between his dark ones like he is holding some delicate, precious bird he has captured and doesn't want to let go.

The other thing I see is Mo'ma's face. She is turned slightly away from the camera, and she is looking up at Sug, my great grampa, like she is seeing God and Jesus and all the Saints, her head tilted back, face shining, hair rippling wild down her back .

and there is something in the way she looks that makes me want to cry.

Mo'ma begins to rock again. "You know, child," she says after a while, almost too soft for me to hear, "on our weddin' night, himself braided up my hair."

Wheezer

"Raymond! Raymond, come out here. Now!"

Ray jolted awake, pain shooting up the back of his neck as his head snapped forward. He knew that tone - it was the one Doris used whenever she was gearing up for a major fit, and this one, judging from the decibel level she'd already achieved, would be a humdinger.

Ray struggled to his feet, as rapidly as his arthritis would allow. His recliner had seen better days, and every time Doris got the bug to refurbish, he lived in fear that she would fixate on it and suggest they buy a new one. If he'd learned any one thing after forty-two years of marriage, it was that with a woman like Doris, a man had to stay alert for changing conditions.

Ray shuffled to the kitchen doorway. Doris stood with her back against the sink, arms folded tightly across her midriff, glaring at the kitchen floor, where a large, yellow pool marred the gleam of freshly waxed tile. Across the room, wedged beneath the safety of the kitchen table, lay Wheezer, his rheumy brown eyes darting worriedly from Doris to Ray and back again.

It was hard to say just what sort of unholy coupling had produced Wheezer. His build hinted at collie, with a trace of Airedale, and something that was almost, but not quite, Labrador. His coat leaned toward Shepherd, Malamute and possibly Bouvier - his eyebrows definitely Schnauzer - his coloring Palomino tan and dingy white. When Ray had first seen him, peering out over the edge of a large cardboard box in Lester Wilmes' toolshed, it occurred to Ray that he was not much to look at - but, then, neither was Ray. Looks weren't everything, and there was something about the way that pup held his head, cocked slightly to one side, that made Ray wonder if the little fella wasn't a good deal smarter than he looked, so Ray took him home.

Doris had not been impressed.

"For goodness' sake, Ray," she'd said, wiping her hands on a kitchen towel as she inspected the little mutt sticking his head out of Ray's denim jacket. "You could at least have gotten a dog that looks like a REAL dog. That little thing doesn't look like anything I ever saw. And what's wrong with him, anyway? Why's he breathing like that - is he sick?"

The minute Doris patted the pup tentatively on his pointed little head, he began to suck air like a drowning sailor. Ray stared down at him.

"I dunno," Ray said. "He seemed all right at Lester's." He'd put the pup down on the floor where he began the traditional Dog Dance of Ecstasy, wriggling his behind so frantically that both ends of dog almost met one another, wheezing loudly and dribbling with uncontainable delight as he thrashed across the kitchen floor. Doris had frowned and reached for the paper towels.

In the twelve ensuing years, Wheezer had done little to endear himself to Doris. While Ray found the rattle of his breathing rather soothing, like white noise, Doris had banished him from the bedroom early on, and the dog's other habits ranged from the mildly annoying (yipping and twitching his paws when he slept, dreaming, no doubt, of chasing rabbits,) to the inexcusable (lying on his back in the living room and emitting clouds of exquisitely odiferous flatulence whenever there were guests). Now that

Wheezer was getting on in age, she seemed to take his occasional lapses of bladder control as a personal affront.

Now, she shot Ray a look brimming with accusation.

"I'm telling you, Raymond, I can't take much more of this. That dog is either going to have to stay outside, or it's time to take him to Doc Taylor's. I will NOT have him wetting all over this house. I just mopped the floor Tuesday, and look at it! Now I'll have to do the whole thing over again!"

Ray would have liked to suggest to Doris that he'd just mop up the puddle and run a damp sponge over the spot, but that would have been like suggesting to Custer that the Indians should be left alone. He knew that Doris would not be happy until she'd redone the entire floor. She probably wouldn't be happy then, either, but at least she might reach the state of grim satisfaction that, for Doris, passed as happiness.

"C'mon, boy," Ray said to Wheezer, a little more sharply than he meant to. Wheezer swam out from under the table on the slick tile and floundered to his feet, tail tucked apologetically between his legs. Ray grabbed his windbreaker and Wheezer's leash off the hook by the back door, and the two of them trudged out onto the back porch and down the steps into the late afternoon October sun.

Lately Doris had been getting on Ray's last remaining nerve, a process that surprised him. He thought she'd successfully done that years ago, but this was the third time she'd mentioned Doc Taylor in as many weeks, and Ray just didn't want to hear it. He knew what she meant, all right - the Last Trip to the Vet, who would administer the Big Sleep. Just because Wheezer had a little trouble containing himself was no reason to jump the gun. Heck, Ray had trouble himself now and then - some nights he'd considered just sleeping in the bathroom, to save having to get up six or seven times, but that was what happened when you got older. Sometimes he wondered if he was next on Doris' hit list..

Ray and Wheezer looked at one another for a moment, then set off in silent agreement for the pond. It was a long hike - they hadn't been there since early last spring, Ray thought, but it might be good for him to get some exercise for his stiff knees, and Wheezer could pretend to hunt, which was what Wheezer liked best in the world.

Ray had known right off that Wheezer was a different kind of a dog. They were still farming then, and Ray started training Wheezer just like he'd trained all the other dogs to go fetch in the cows for milking. They'd gone together a few times, with Ray encouraging Wheezer loudly, with "C'mon, dog, let's go get 'em. Round 'em up, boy!" Wheezer had been delighted, zooming around the pasture in a blurr of orange and white fur, stampeding the cows toward Ray till he'd had to take refuge behind a sapling - but the first time he opened the pasture gate and urged Wheezer to "Go get 'em" while he stayed behind in the barnyard, Wheezer had lunged a few yards down the path, noticed that Ray was not behind him, and sat down. He'd looked over his shoulder at Ray expectantly, wagging his ridiculously ratty tail, his ears shifting position like antennae, and nothing would induce him to move until Ray came along.

Bill Heller, who'd stopped by to borrow something, had shook his head. "That sure ain't no cow dog," he'd said mournfully, dismissing Wheezer. Ray had found himself unreasonably irritated. Everybody in the neighborhood knew that Bill Heller was a moron - he'd once run over his foot with his own tractor - but there was more to it than that. Wheezer was not stupid - he was just independent, a trait lots of folks didn't truly appreciate. .

Take the squirrel incident, for example. Along about the time Wheezer was a year old, a squirrel had chewed a hole in the garage, up under the eaves, and was nesting in there. Ray had tried everything - mothballs, nailing tin over the hole - he thought about shooting the darned thing, but killing things was hard for Ray to stomach, bad trait for a farmer, but there it was. He'd come around the side of the garage one afternoon with Wheezer right behind him, just in time to see the squirrel shinnying down the drainpipe, snotty as you please.

"Dang squirrel," Ray shouted.

Wheezer had looked at Ray, eyebrows working quizzically, then at the squirrel, and suddenly he took off after that sucker so fast that Ray couldn't see anything but a blur going across the backyard. Treed that squirrel as nicely as any hound dog Ray had ever come across, then laid down by the foot of the tree, and that was that. Come supper time, dog wouldn't come in when Ray called him - had to feed him out by the foot of the tree. Fact was for the next two days Wheezer hunkered down by the corner of the garage just waiting for that squirrel to show up so's he could run it off. From there on, all Ray had to say was "squirrel," and Wheezer would be off after it like a shot. True, he never actually caught one, but his tenacity pleased Ray.

Ray looked over his shoulder. Wheezer was snorting along a few feet behind him, examining the dry fall ground cover.

"Hey, boy!" Ray said. Wheezer didn't look up.

Hey, Boy!" He yelled a little louder. Wheezer raised his head and gave a perfunctory wag of his tail. He snarfled happily at Ray, a rasping sound like an electric fan with something caught in the blades.

It was a perfect afternoon to sit by the pond. A few years ago, before his ticker had gone bad, Ray had hauled the back seat of an old Buick out there one afternoon and set it on the bank of the pond, facing West. Sitting there, the sun hit you just right in the afternoon, and Ray could look off toward the home place and dream dreams of things that had already come to pass. He couldn't actually see the old farmstead, of course, but just knowing it was off there in the distance made him feel better sometimes. Doris, who hated getting her white tennis shoes dirty, had never been back to the pond since the day the realtor showed them the place, so Ray had claimed it as a haven of solitude where he could retreat from the unrelenting tidiness of home.

Ray missed the farm. It had been hard work, backbreaking work, but he had never thought of doing anything else. The first signs of green washing the tips of the trees in spring, the way the sun hit a field of ripe wheat, turning it into a sea of gold - in truth, the only reason Ray had bought this place, instead of one of those little crackerbox houses in town that Doris favored, was because a man needed some land to put his feet down on.

It was one of those rare fall days, breezy but still warm enough to be outdoors. When they reached the stand of maples and scrub oak that circled the eastern shore of the pond, the leaves crackled beneath Ray's feet, and the rich smell of loam rose up to greet him.

Suddenly, off to Ray's left, there was the sharp snap of a twig breaking. Ray stopped short. Last spring, he and Wheezer had seen a pair of whitetails standing among the trees. The male, still working his jaw on a mouthful of tree bark, had stared at them for what seemed like a full minute or so before he caught Ray's scent and he and the doe bounded off through the brush. It had been quite a sight.

Slowly Ray turned his head in the direction of the sound. At first he saw nothing, then, halfway down the trunk of an old, dead elm, he spotted it - a fat, plume-tailed grey squirrel, cheeks puffed with supplies for winter storage. Its tail flicked angrily at the interruption in its gathering routine. Behind him in the brush, Wheezer's crashing advance suddenly halted.

Ray turned slightly. Wheezer had spotted the squirrel, too. His gaze darted from the squirrel to Ray and back again, eyes pleading with Ray for permission. Ray saw that Wheezer's hindquarters were trembling with the intensity of his desire.

What the heck, Ray thought to himself. Sometimes you just gotta do what you gotta do.

"Squirrel, Wheezer," he said in a quiet voice, but before the words had passed his lips, Wheezer was mobilized, thrashing toward the tree, a whirlwind of leaves flying in his wake.

If the squirrel had been smart, which Ray had expected, it would have headed back up the tree. Instead, made brazen by too much testosterone, or perhaps merely desperate to reach home with the spoils, the furry fiend made a run for it, shooting down the tree and tearing off through the trees with Wheezer in hot pursuit.

"Dang!" Ray said to himself. 'Wheezer! WHEEZER! C'mere boy!"

The thrashing receded in the distance.

"Dagnabbit Wheezer," Ray shouted. "You're too old for this nonsense, and I'm too old to chase after you. COME BACK HERE!"

Ray heard a yelp, then another, fainter.

Sighing, he turned and made his way through the trees to the edge of the pond. Darn dog would just have to handle this on his own. He hated to admit it, but the walk had been a little more than he was used to. He sank gratefully onto the Buick seat and stared out at the pond.

Five or ten minutes passed, then another ten or so. Ray was beginning to get a mite uneasy. If Wheezer had treed that squirrel, he just might be bone headed enough to stay there, thinking Ray would come looking for him. He shifted position, and was just struggling to his feet, when he heard rustling in the underbrush.

Wheezer staggered through the weeds slowly, stopping every

few feet to pull in a breath and sounding like a locomotive running on damp coal. Ray stood, slapped his leg.

"Wheezer, you dumb mutt," Ray said. "C'mere, boy. Did you get 'im? Did ya?"

Wheezer dragged himself painfully over to Ray, his tail giving a few brief swipes in the affirmative. He leaned against Ray's leg, chest heaving, and looked up at him sheepishly.

Ray sank back down onto the seat and Wheezer clambered up beside him, sinking down with a heavy sigh..

"Old fool," Ray muttered, but he reached over to rub the dog's bony head as he leaned back against the sun-warmed upholstery.

Lulled by the sunshine and the reassuring rasp of Wheezer's breathing, Ray dozed.

When he awoke, the sun had all but disappeared on the horizon, and it took a minute or two before Ray realized that it was still.

Too still.

Ray sat by the pond for a long time. The sky went from blue to gold, magenta and deep violet, then on to blue again, but a deeper this time. It was a beautiful sunset, Ray guessed, as sunsets went, but his vision was too blurred by tears to see it very clearly, and the unbroken silence formed a cold, hard knot in the center of his chest.

Tak Jest

TAK JEST JAK JEST.

It is what it is.

It was Lina's Polish grandmother's favorite saying. When Lina was younger it seemed meaningless to her, just another of the old country platitudes, but over the years she has come to appreciate the simple philosophy.

Some nights it is a soothing mantra, nights when your back and shoulders ache from carrying the heavy serving trays, your face is tight from smiling, when even the piano music drifting from the bar grates on your nerves. Lina often finds herself watching the faces of customers light with pleasure at the first notes of a familiar melody and wonders what they would think if they knew how often she has heard that same tune, how it feels burned into her brain the way David's criticism once did. Funny that while he loved to remind her what a bad mother she was, he never asked for custody of the kids, didn't even bother to see them after the divorce.

Most of the time now, when she thinks of him at all, Lina believes that David was wrong. At forty-eight, her body is beginning to show signs of wear from all the hours on her feet, but she still fits into the same size uniform she wore when she started, and she can still handle the work. Maybe waitressing isn't brain surgery, but she's done OK, managed to raise Mark and Jillian on her salary plus tips and, and they've turned out fine.

It is early on a Thursday evening, no customers at Lina's tables yet, so Karen agrees to watch while she slips off to the bathroom for a moment. As she dries her hands under the electric blower Lina appraises herself in the mirror. The skin on her neck is dry and crepey and her hair looks tired, dull. It shouldn't matter, it really doesn't matter, she just has to be nice to the customers for the next six hours, but she feels old tonight, old and tired to the bone. She tightens the laces on her bodice, gives a last tug to the dirndl skirt to smooth it over her hips and returns to the floor.

There's a new customer, Karen tells her, rolling her eyes toward the small, two-person table in the alcove off the bar, and Lina goes immediately to the table to introduce herself.

"Good evening sir, my name is Lina and I'll be your server this evening. Can I get you a beverage to start off with?"

The man blinks up at her, startled, colors and quickly drops his eyes to the safety of the menu. He is perhaps in his fifties, pale, with thinning black hair cropped close in a careless cut, and he is startlingly fat. His chin drapes over the collar of his worn, stained polo shirt, and Lina can see that his body puddles into the chair, belly lapping over his thighs beneath the table. Even his fingers are fat sausages, creased at the knuckles, yet oddly graceful as he points at the list of entrees.

"This," he gestures at the pork hock baked with sauerkraut. "Is it big? How big is it?"

"It's large, sir," Lina replies. "A very generous serving, and it comes with the kraut and a potato dumpling." She is about to make the standard response that most customers cannot finish it but hesitates, not wanting to make him feel uncomfortable. Lina has learned in this job to be careful of the feelings of total strangers.

"Soup or salad, too?"

"Yes, all entrees come with soup or salad."

"Can I have stuffing instead of the sauerkraut?" he asks. This time he makes brief eye contact with her, his look hopeful.

Inside her head Lina can hear the chef grousing at her as he always does when asked to do a substitution.

"I believe we can do that for you, sir," Lina nods.

"Oh, good, very good," he says. "And bread, you'll bring bread, hot bacon dressing on the salad, extra if they'll let you do that, and can I have some coffee while I'm waiting?"

"Of course, sir, I'll get your coffee right away."

"With cream, please. Is it real cream?"

"Yes it is, sir."

The man is nodding rapidly, a pleased expression on his face. There is something childlike about him, Lina thinks as she picks up the bread from the kitchen, plops a salad on her tray and grabs a coffee pot from the service bar. She pours his coffee, sets the bread board carefully on the outer edge of the table, and places the salad in front of him.

"Mmmmmmm yes, warm bread. Very good," he murmurs.

Lina overhears one of the customers at another table complaining that it is snowing hard outside. That means business will probably be slow tonight. Usually Lina likes being busy, it means better tips and the evenings go faster, but tonight it would be nice to catch a break.

Despite his complaints, the chef is very conscientious about timing, and it is not long before the fat man's order is plated and ready for pickup.

He looks up as Lina approaches with the tray, and his face is transformed with pleasure.

"Ahhhh, yes," he croons as Lina settles the plate before him. "Beautiful, beautiful!" He tucks his napkin into his shirt collar, carefully picks up his knife and fork. Lina usually asks if there is anything more she can do for the customer, but it is clear that he is focused on the food, so Lina returns the tray to the kitchen and continues with other tasks.

The standard of service is to approach the customer midway through dinner to check on whether anything else might be needed, but Lina finds herself reluctant, even though it is quiet in the restaurant and she has time. She watches the fat man from her station near the bar, and he is completely absorbed by his meal, lips shining with grease, fingertips picking delicately at the mound of meat in front of him, so intimately engaged that it seems somehow indecent to interrupt.

Karen raises an eyebrow at Lina as she waits for the decaf coffee to finish dripping at the service bay.

"Glad *you* got him," she murmurs.

Lina shrugs. There is something oddly mesmerizing about the way the fat man is enjoying his meal. Lina cannot remember enjoying a meal like that, except perhaps when she was small. When he leans back at last, patting his lips with the napkin, Lina feels comfortable enough to approach his table.

"Can I get you anything else, sir? Some dessert?"

He pauses as if considering, then nods.

"Do you have cheesecake?"

"Yes, we do sir, plain or with cherries or blueberries."

"With cherries. I would like to take it with me." he says.

"Very good, sir, I'll get that for you right away. More coffee?"

He declines, and Lina goes to pick up the cheesecake, makes out the bill and slips the folder onto the corner of his table as unobtrusively as possible as she presents him with the dessert.

"Here you are, sir," Lina says, "and thank you very much for dining with us."

The fat man looks up at Lina, and suddenly he is focused on

her as if seeing her fully for the first time. The look is intense, disconcerting.

"Thank you," he says, slipping a credit card into the folder and handing it back to her. He does not look at the bill. "Add on your tip, twenty per cent."

Lina smiles her thanks. As she walks back to the bar with the folder, Karen grimaces at Lina but Lina pretends not to see. She has had a lot of odd customers over the years, and she is not repelled, as Karen seems to be, but simply curious at this sadly unkempt man dining alone in such an exclusive place.

He is on his feet when Lina returns with his card. He thanks her, shyly pockets the card in his tattered winter jacket and lumbers past her toward the exit.

Lina is used to the detritus of extravagant meals, pools of melted ice cream, napkins streaked with grease and lipstick, heaps of bone and gristle, but looking at the fat man's table she finds a peculiar neatness. The napkin is folded and laid beneath the fork to the left of the plate, the other pieces of silver returned to the original place setting - even the skin peeled from the pork shank is meticulously folded into a square and placed atop the bones on the bread plate. It is, somehow, a polite gesture, a kindness, leaving the table as neat as possible.

Two Thursdays later the fat man appears at the same time. It is a typically busy night, but the alcove table has just been vacated, and again Lina finds herself waiting on him. He is once more intent on the menu, asking Lina if the hunter's sauce is made with real butter, is the asparagus fresh, can he have extra cream for his coffee, and perhaps spaetzle rather than cabbage. It becomes a ritual that is repeated every other Thursday night. Even though Lina has already learned the fat man's name from his credit card, he introduces himself to her as Steven Velos. He always asks for the alcove table, perhaps Lina thinks because it is in a dark corner and he feels embarrassed that he is so shabbily dressed, but he does not mind waiting, is never rude or cross if the service is slow, and he is always a generous tipper. Gradually he becomes slightly more comfortable, Lina notices. Sometimes he smiles when Lina addresses him as Mr. Velos, and slowly he begins to speak to her, a comment now and then about the weather, the music, or perhaps some neutral bit of news. Lina also notices that sometimes when he thinks she will not notice, he looks at her breasts. This is something Lina has learned to endure over the years, but it does not happen often as it used to. His wistful glances remind Lina of a boy who once liked her in middle school, sweet but far too shy to approach her.

Mr Velos never seems to tire of the menu, and his eyes light with excitement at the arrival of each order.

"Exquisite!" he exclaims. "Perfect!" He spends several moments simply observing the food, tucking the napkin into his frayed collar, touching his water glass, the bread plate, the silver approvingly before he begins to eat.

He rarely orders dessert, but Lina always offers, and when he does accept it is with a kind of guilty glee.

"I shouldn't, you know, I really shouldn't" he says coyly, shaking his head, "but yes, I believe I will."

Gradually, Lina finds herself anticipating these Thursday visits. Mr. Velos is consistently polite and so predictable that if he misses his regular evening she finds herself wondering what might have happened.

One Thursday Lina has to switch shifts with another server so he can go to the dentist.

"You should have been here last night," Karen tells her the next evening. "The fat guy who always asks for table six was here as usual, and he pitched a fit because you weren't on. 'Where is she?' he wants to know. 'Will she be in later, is she sick?' Made me feel really creepy. I got Jeff to wait on him, and Jeff said he complained all evening, was a real pain. I don't know how you can deal with it."

Lina shrugs. "He's not so bad once you get to know him," she says, realizing even as she says it that she doesn't know him, not really.

Summer comes, and there is the usual slowdown, people leaving town for vacations, eating at cafes that offer outdoor dining. On Thursdays there are hardly any customers, but the restaurant stays open, and tonight it is so slow that Lina only has two tables, a group of four in town for the Fourth of July and Steven Velos. He orders duck this evening, a heavy meal for such a hot evening, and Lina suggests something cold to drink, not his usual coffee. After a moment's thought he nods agreement.

"You're very nice to me, Miss Lina" he says when she brings his iced tea. He speaks tentatively as though afraid he will mispronounce her name. Lina notices that he blushes as he says it and she finds this oddly touching.

"You are a good customer, sir. You're always polite . . ." He is gazing at her expectantly, and Lina can feel that he wants to have a conversation.

"So, will you go to the fireworks tomorrow night?"

"The fireworks," he says, nodding. "I have a perfect view of the fireworks from my apartment. I live on the top floor of the Biltmore Village building, the lake side. All I have to do is open my drapes."

Lina cannot remember when she last saw fireworks. She works most nights, and after David left she could never get off to take the children, so they always went with their friends and other parents.

"Would you like to come and watch them from my window?"

The fat man is flushed, unable to meet her eyes and Lina

understands that the question has been excruciatingly difficult for him to ask.

"Thank you for asking me," Lina finds herself saying. "I work the early shift tomorrow, but I would like that, yes."

His face is suffused with pleasure. He will meet her, he says excitedly, here in front of the restaurant at 8:30 pm. They will have time to walk back to his apartment, which is only four blocks away. His delight is palpable.

When Lina finishes her shift the next evening and steps out of the front entrance to the restaurant, Steven Velos is there, waiting, dark circles of sweat staining the armpits of his sport shirt.

"Hello. Was it crowded tonight? Were you busy? Let's walk this way, up here a block and two more over." He gestures the way to Lina.

"Sorry," she tells him. "I didn't have time to change. I hope that's all right."

"Yes, yes it's fine," he reassures her, glancing toward her without making eye contact.

"I like your uniform. It's . . . it makes you look very nice."

It is wickedly hot and humid, and Lina can hear the man's labored breathing between the bursts of nervous chatter he makes as they walk. When they reach the building Lina stops and looks up, surprised. The building is tall, imposing, and Mr Velos gestures upward.

"That's where I live, the top floor," he says. "It's not much, a small apartment, like an efficiency. I take my meals out, the main ones . . ."

He babbles on nervously as they enter the cool, softly lit lobby, passing the huge marble fireplace, damask upholstered wing chairs, pots of fan palms, real ones, not silk, and beautifully cared for.

"Well, here we are," Steven Velos says breathlessly, fumbling for the key in his pants pocket when they reach the top floor. "As I told you, it's really not much, rather small."

He swings the door open and Lina steps through, hearing him flip the light switch behind her.

The room is wide, made seemingly wider by the large window that opens the wall ahead of her to the night sky, and Lina is astonished. The walls are a deep shade of cinnabar red, and in one corner of the room is an Oriental table, inlaid with ornate designs in mother-of-pearl and ivory. Against the wall to her left a mahogany armoire gleams darkly. A carved grey marble cat sleeps at the base of the long, low chaise beneath the window, a luxurious aubergine velvet throw draping across the foot, gold tassels teasing the cat's back - and the light! It curls into the room like sweet gold smoke, pouring from the translucent glass bowl of an ornate Victorian lamp, a bronze of a seminude woman with a mass of wavy hair holding the shade aloft. The furnishings do not match, yet each piece has been chosen with great care to fit its place, and the effect is stunning.

Lina walks further into the room, exhaling finally, the sound of awe.

"You like it." The man is pleased, smiling widely, and he gestures toward the walls, the top of the armoire, the windowsill. "The pictures are of my family, myself and my family."

Every available surface, Lina sees, holds pictures, beautifully framed old snapshots taken long ago. In one a plain-faced, smiling couple stand one on either side of a small boy, dark and stockily built. In succeeding pictures. the boy grows, taking up more and more space in each photo as the parents age, seeming to shrink as the boy expands, finally disappearing. Atop the armoire there is one formal portrait of the boy, grown to a large, broad-shouldered young man with a handsome face, seated in a high-school graduation pose and smiling stiffly at the camera. It is obviously Steven Velos, much younger but still with the same shyness in his eyes.

"They are very nice pictures," Lina says kindly. "And your home is so elegant."

"I like beautiful things," he says, almost apologetically, walking around her to drop heavily on the chaise beneath the window, facing her but looking down and away. "It's why I go there, you know, to the restaurant. For the wonderful food - and to look at you."

He looks up then, almost fearfully, his cheeks flushed. The fireworks are beginning outside the window, but his eyes are locked on her, worshipful, yearning.

Lina watches the rockets hiss upward and explode in flashes of blue, green, gold, cascades of color, and she smiles at the loudness, the sheer flamboyance.

It is what it is, Lina thinks. She feels the man's fingers, tentative at first, loosening the black satin ribbon at her bodice, then unzipping the skirt, letting each piece fall to the floor as they do on nights when she herself is simply too tired to hang them up properly.

The light from outside the window plays across her skin, glinting apricot and gold and she steps forward, closer to the man.

"Oh my, lovely, so lovely," he breathes. His hand, trembling, touches her hip, his face leaning in to press against her belly as the fireworks splash across the sky, so beautiful that Lina is not sure where to look, so after a time she simply closes her eyes.

The Gate

I THOUGHT I HEARD THE GATE A MINUTE AGO, BUT IT MUST HAVE been the wind.

I'd get up and look, but I'm so tired these days and one of the kittens is on my lap and I hate to disturb them.

Sometimes my neighbor, Anna, comes by to bring me some soup or just to check on me, but she's almost eighty and doesn't get around well herself.

The house we grew up in didn't have a gate, not even a true fenced yard, just a long spread of some grass and trees that stretched out to the gravel road, but we played there and it was fine. We didn't have much, what with Da going off on the drink like he did when there was no work for him on the boats, but we were always fine till Davy fell out of the big pine tree when he was seven.

I heard him yell, and it was different from when the boys were just playing, there was fear in it, and pain. I ran as fast as I could, but Mam got there first. He was laying on the ground, his leg bent in a shape I'd never seen before, and he was crying, something he never did.

"It's broken," Mam said. "We'll have to get him to the doctor. Have Sam and James Arthur hitch up the horses."

I was the oldest girl, just sixteen, so Mam had me drive the wagon while she sat with Davy. The roads were rough, then, and it was a long way to Ephriam, but there was only one doctor on the whole peninsula. When we got there, I tied up the horse, ran in and told a man who was sitting in the waiting room about Davy. He went out and helped carry him in, took him right through into the office and put him on a table, Mam and me trailing behind.

I can still remember the first time I laid eyes on Louis. He was tall, solid, with wide shoulders and big, capable hands, his dark hair combed back from his face in waves, a thread of silver here and there at the temples. He looked at Mam, then me, asked what happened and bent over Davy, his face serious. I felt frozen, not just from the shock of the accident, but something else, something I couldn't name because I'd never felt it before.

"His leg is broken, we'll have to set it as soon as possible," he told Mam. "I can give him some paregoric, but it's still going to hurt. You'll need to hold him as still as possible. Mother, you come over on this side, and you, miss -"

"Mae," I said, stepping to Davy's other side. I took his cold little hand, warming it in mine while Mam talked softly to him as the doctor prepared. He nodded when he was ready, and Mam looked away, but I had an idea.

"Davy, remember when you and Billy caught that big brown trout in October? Tell me about it again."

It was the biggest thing that had ever happened to Davy, and he was still excited about it a year later.

"Come on, then," I urged. "I bet the doctor never heard a story like that. He'll want to hear it, for sure."

"I surely would. Don't get much chance to fish myself, and I love a good fisherman's yarn."

Davy began to talk, and Mam and I held him tight while Louis set the leg. He cried out once or twice, but Louis appeared so interested in his tale that it kept Davy distracted. When the leg was set, all of us were exhausted. Mam bent her head and rested it on the table, and Louis looked at me then. I had Da's hair, red and flyaway, and I hadn't had time to pin it up properly before we left home. I must have looked a fright, but it didn't matter, because everything fell away and there was just Louis, his grey eyes looking into mine.

Mam spoke, and Louis turned to her quickly.

"We will pay you, sir," Mam said. "My husband, Thomas Devlin, works on the boats, and it's scarce right now, but we will pay, soonest we can."

Louis nodded. "Not to worry, mother," he said. "If I might ask, your daughter here, is she done with schooling?"

Mam nodded. "A good student, too."

"I'm asking because she has a way about her with people," Louis said. "I have been looking for an assistant, someone to keep the books, help with patients and the like. My wife is expecting again, and we have a son at home, so it's too much for her. If you could spare your daughter to do some work for me it would be most helpful, and we might come to an arrangement for my services. I will need to see Davy again, so perhaps you could talk it over with your husband and let me know."

"Yes!" I said. Mam looked at me sharply. "Yes, I'll come to work for you."

Both of them were taken aback, I think, by how forward I was, but Louis nodded.

"If your parents agree to it, he said. "The bookkeeping is relatively simple, my wife can show you, and I can give you some instruction on caring for patients. You're not put off by the sight of blood, I hope?"

I had to smile. "There's not a week goes by but what my brothers don't bash themselves up some way or another. They're a rough lot."

"Good," Louis said. He gave Mam a syrup to give Davy for the first few days to lessen the pain, told us what to watch for while he healed, and said he would come by in two weeks to check on the leg.

There were six of us at home then, and even though I loved my brothers and sisters I was ready to have a life of my own. Back in those days you married and had your own family, it was just what you did, but having a job? A real job, where I got to learn things and get paid? It sounded like heaven.

I think about Davy and the rest of them now and then. Davy had a bit of a limp till the day he died, but he was lucky, had a good life, a nice wife - I still see her on occasion. The others moved far and away, except for Charlotte. She's in Bailey's Harbor, ornery as ever. For a long while we didn't speak - at first I thought she was jealous that I had a job, made my own way, but later I realized it was just pure judgement. She shamed me for years, until she finally realized I never was ashamed.

My first few weeks of work were hard. I'm good with numbers, but I hated the bookkeeping. It was simple, really, just a ledger, and Louis' wife Inger taught me everything I needed to know. Louis saw patients in the Ephraim office on Mondays and Wednesdays and did house calls the rest of the week, so I only worked three days, billing, answering the phone and making appointments. It was dull, but I kept myself busy with my sketchbook in between times.

When Mrs. Anders came in that Tuesday afternoon in October, I could see   something was wrong right off. She was clutching her back, pale and sweaty, bent over her huge belly. Her eldest daughter and I helped her to a chair, but she was in a bad way.

"It's too early," she moaned. "Baby's not due for two weeks, doctor said."

"Is it your first?" I asked.

My second," she told me. I knew about babies coming, had helped Mom with Sam and Charlotte, but this was different.

"Let's get you laid down," I said. "Doctor is out on calls, but maybe I can find someone to help."

Hardly anyone had phones then, so I sent her daughter to run to the mercantile and see if they could call the midwife who lived in town, but she didn't answer, by then Mrs Anders was in full on labor, and I figured no one else was coming to help. I had her daughter put the kettle on for hot water, cleaned her up, got some blankets and sheets ready and did what I could for her.

When the baby finally came out, he was tiny and not crying.

"Is the baby all right?" Mrs. Anders kept asking, but I didn't have time to answer her.

I wiped him off with warm, wet cloths, cleaned out his nose and mouth, but he still wasn't moving. All I could think to do was rub his chest and back to warm him, and I blew in his face, gently, then harder. I thought he was gone, but suddenly he jerked, sucked in a breath, and started wailing.

"You have a boy," I told Mrs. Anders. I swaddled him in blankets and put him on his mother's chest.

I wonder if that was when things began to change, or if what happened would have happened anyway. When Louis got back to the office, Mrs. Anders was sleeping, and her daughter had gone to fetch her father. The baby had nursed a little and was dozing in my arms when Louis walked in. He set his bag on the chair by the door, and stopped dead.

"Mae? What's this, then?"

I couldn't stop smiling. "Mrs. Anders decided to have her wee one a bit early," I said. "The midwife was away somewhere, and I couldn't reach you."

He walked over, took the baby from me, turned the blankets

back and looked him over carefully, fingers, toes, the umbilical cord where I'd tied it off.

"You did well, Mae, very well," he told me.

When the Anders family was safely away home and the office was empty, Louis came and stood in front of me.

"Mae," he said solemnly, "you are a wonder." He took a lock of my hair between his fingers, stroking it gently, brushed it back into place, and my knees went weak.

I believe I had loved Louis from the moment I saw his face, but it was then that I understood that my heart had no room for anyone but him.

"Come, I'll take you home in my car tonight," he said abruptly, stepping back. "You've had a very busy day. Your mother will be rightly proud to hear what you've accomplished."

She was, and Da was too, although he made light of it as usual. When Louis suggested that I work more days and do house calls with him, they barely blinked. I was taking most of my earnings home, and with winter coming on it would be a great help.

I learned so much from Louis - how to suture a simple wound, how to deliver a breach baby, setting broken bones, what to do for a fever. It was good to be useful, but mostly I was just happy being with him. We talked about everything on those car trips, mostly medicine because I had endless questions, but when we both fell silent the air around us felt sacred.

It was a bad winter that first year, heavy snows every few days, and a lot of people had influenza and the like. Mostly we managed, but sometimes the snow was too deep for Louis to drive, so had to see patients at the office if they could get there by horse and buggy. Right after New Year's a terrible bad blizzard hit about ten in the morning, and by one o'clock, Louis knew he couldn't get home in the car.

"I'll see to whoever comes in, Mae," he told me. Maybe Mrs. Frey has a spare room over at the boarding house you can sleep in tonight. You surely can't walk home in this."

"It's all right," I told him. "Mam will know I stayed in town. She already told me not to try walking home if it gets bad."

We still had two patients that afternoon, but only one showed, and by 4:00 pm it was dark and the snow outside was wicked, wind off the bay thrumming at the windows.

"I'm going to lock up," Louis said.

"I'll put the kettle on," I told him. "There's tea in the cupboard in the storeroom, and some of that bread Mrs. Davis brought when they came in Monday."

"Did you call Mrs. Frey?"

I didn't answer. Louis turned the sign on the door to 'Closed,' pulled the shade down and turned to look at me.

I was trembling inside, not knowing exactly what I wanted, only that I wanted it more than anything. I shook my head.

"I will stay here," I said. "With you."

Along with all that came later; the gossip, the shunning, the sheer meanness, there were some who said that Louis took advantage of me. I never cared about any of it but that, blaming him for something that I had wrought. That one thing angered me, made me spiteful so as never to speak to those who I knew had said it.

I walked the miles across the room to him then, put my hands to his shoulders, nestled my face into his chest, breathing in the scent of him as though I were drowning and he was the air.

"Ah, Mae," he said, so soft. "Are you sure of this, really sure?"

I nodded, stepped in closer, and he put a hand up to cup my head, the other about my waist. We began.

It took some time before the talk started to float about, but eventually it did. Men may see what women do - a certain look, a brief touch - but they keep it to themselves. Women, though, will talk. I paid as little heed as possible and went about my business, in church every Sunday nodding politely to the other parishoners, even those who wouldn't speak. Mam finally heard something, though, probably because my little sister Charlotte brought some particular tidbit home from town, and she spoke to me.

"Mae, sit down. There are rumors going round about you and the doctor," Mam said, putting a cup of tea in front of me. "Do you know about this?"

I nodded "There's always somebody who will start talk for the pleasure of it, even if there's nothing to talk about."

Mam shook her head. "You need to stop, my girl. I see the way you smile at one another, the joy in your face when he comes down the road. You need to stop now, before something happens you'll regret."

I looked at her steadily for a moment, and she knew.

I wouldn't say we fought, not really, because I never spoke a word in my defense. Mam railed at me, the terrible example I was setting for my sisters, the shame it would bring to the family. It might be bringing shame, but it was also bringing a few dollars that were desperately needed. Da couldn't be counted on regularly for the bills, and there was not a thing a young woman like myself could do that would pay as well in the whole of the peninsula. I let Mam carry on till she ran short of words, then got up and went to fire up the wood stove.

Eventually, of course, Louis heard things, too. When he asked me about it, I would not lie, I could never lie to Louis, and he was more angry than sad.

"Do your parents know?"

"Mam was on me about it, but I let it roll off me," I said, which was only a little true. "She won't tell Da on account of his temper."

"We need," he began.

"I need a place of my own," I said firmly. I knew what he was thinking to say, that we needed to stop being together. I took his hand between mine.

"I am all right," I said. "It will be all right," and it was, because I willed it so.

Eden Farmer, the ragged old man who had a shack up behind the Lutheran church, was a drinker like my Da, and it finally did him in. When one of the congregation found him, he'd been with God for some time and the place was in awful shape, full of flies, old papers, rotting food, the remains of a sad life. No one wanted the place, and there was talk of tearing it down, but no one stepped up to do the job.

Louis said no outright when I told him my plan.

"The place is falling down, Mae," he said. "It's only two rooms with an outhouse in back. I doubt there's even a deed for it."

"The church owns the land," I told him. "They need money for repairs, and it's a nice, quiet spot. I would be close to the office, too. I should think they'd be glad to have it off their hands."

It took me some time to convince him, and maybe I never would have, but Da got wind of the rumors and came home full of drink and rage. We had an awful row, and though Mam tried to quiet him for the little ones' sake, he roared down the wrath of the Almighty on me and slapped me so hard I flew into the wall.

After he fell into a drunken sleep I put my few clothes into a carpetbag, kissed Mam and told her not to fret, and walked into town.

The next morning Louis found me asleep on the cot in the office, with a dark bruise on my cheekbone. He was furious, but I told him it was bound to come, and after a long conversation he agreed to my idea. I'd been holding some of my wages back, and I approached a church elder I knew, asking to buy Eden's old place. In time the elders decided on a fair price, a bit more than what I'd saved, and Louis gave me the extra.

It took me nearly two years to get this house habitable. Louis got one of the men who owed him for services to put in a door and one new window, but everything else I did myself, a bit at a time. I slept on the floor the first few months, scrounged a chair here, a table there, but it was a happy time for all that, because Louis would come now and then when the office was closed, and fill the empty space with himself.

Those hours are clearer in my mind now than what I did last month, last week, yesterday. I worked most days with Louis, settled in, made a life. I'd like to say the gossip died down, but of course it didn't. Things just went beneath the surface, the way they do in small towns like ours. I was good at my job, and got some grudging respect for it, mostly because Louis wouldn't stand for anything less, but I had no friends, not really. I grew a little garden out back, read some in medical books Louis lent me. It was Louis who brought me Mink, the kitten. This little one on my lap is a descendant of her, how many generations I can't say.

"You need something to do for yourself, Mae," Louis said one evening. "I hate to see you here alone."

"It's enough," I smiled at him. "Charlotte comes by when she can, I see Mam when Da isn't around, and I run into the boys sometimes in town."

He shook his head. By that time, Louis knew how stubborn I was, but a week or so later he brought me some paints, a new sketchbook and canvasses, three of them. That painting on the wall, the one of the gate, is the very first one I did.

I never wanted a fence, or a gate, but it was the one thing Louis insisted on.

In all our years I never had a thought of other men, but for a time the same could not be said of the men themselves. Louis said

I was beautiful, and perhaps it was so, but I never cared much to hear it, and certainly not from anyone but him. Still, I would get whistles, some would call out, and one night after I'd gone to bed there was pounding on my front door.

I couldn't imagine it was Louis, but perhaps an emergency - I threw on my dressing gown and was halfway to the door when a rough voice on the other side shouted.

"Come out here, you! Show yourself, woman!

I didn't recognize the voice, but I could hear the drink in it. I stopped still, but he must have heard my footfalls.

"Come out here, Doc's whore," he yelled. "Come out here and be generous with the rest of us, why don't you?"

There was a strong lock on my door, and I would have let it be, but I heard him muttering, lurching around outside, and then a rock came through my window.

I snatched the broom up, undid the lock and yanked the door open.

"Go home, you drunken sot," I screamed, loud as I could. "Get off with you!" It took him by surprise, and I swung the broom at him wicked hard like my brothers taught me when we played stickball. I caught him on the arm, and it must have hurt like Hades. He yelped, staggered back, and with another good whack I had him running like the coward he was.

It was then Louis had the fence put up, and the gate. It had a good, strong lock, and Louis and I were the only ones with keys. After that, I would always listen for him at the gate, and there wasn't once my heart didn't lift at the sound.

Things change. I never lock the gate now, the keys are long gone, Louis as well. We had too few years, but what years they were! I painted in the hours when we were apart, just to amuse myself at first, but Louis insisted on showing a canvas to someone in Sturgeon Bay, and soon I was selling my paintings. It made a nice little nest egg, so when Louis decided to retire from the practice I was settled. He was tired then, I could hear it in his voice, and he still came by, but not so often. We would sit, not speaking sometimes, but even that was enough.

I was in my little studio room at the back of the house one afternoon when I heard the gate. It had been a long time, too long, but my breath still quickened as I got up to answer the door.

Louis' oldest son, Josef, stood on the steps, looking down at me. *He has his father's height, his eyes,* I thought, a coldness settling in my chest. I hadn't seen Josef in perhaps fifteen years.

"Miss Mae," he said, gripping his cap in one hand, white knuckled. "I have something for you."

I should have asked him in, but I was unable to move. He handed me Louis' gate key, and a large packet.

I thanked him, automatically. He took a few steps down the walk, turned.

"My father always loved you," he said. "He wanted you to know."

I nodded, not saying that I knew, that I had always known, and watched him walk away. When he was gone from sight I stepped back into the house, closed the door, leaned against it and let the tears come. They still do, ambushing me when I least expect, even though that afternoon seems so long ago.

Louis made sure I was taken care of as best he could. I've had enough to keep the house liveable and myself cared for as long as I'm frugal, and I sell a few paintings in summer. The hole in my heart is another matter - on good days, it is smaller, on bad days a vast, empty cavern - but it is always there.

There's the gate again. I must have dozed off - the kitten is gone. Perhaps the latch is loose, I should go and see. Like everything these days, it's old, may need fixing.

I look out. I blink, look again. It can't be, yet Louis is there, slipping his key into the lock, his grey eyes searching to he see if I am at the window.

He raises his hand, smiling, and I raise mine.

My heart lifts.

Pastoral

THE FIRST TIME REVEREND DOUGLAS CARMODY HEARD THE voice of God he was in the shower, vigorously soaping his armpits - personal fastidiousness, particularly in a man of the cloth, was one of the attributes Doug considered essential.

"Douglas, my boy, I've got a job for you," said the Voice.

Doug had never heard God speak to him before. He had, of course, seen God's work, which one would if one paid attention in life, and there had been numerous times when he had paused while reading the word of God and felt that the particular passage he was reading was meant specifically for him. However, hearing the actual voice of God, which seemed to be coming from somewhere above and just over Doug's right shoulder, disgruntled him so that he dropped the soap.

"Sorry," the Voice said, and emitted a deep chuckle.

Doug could not immediately recall anywhere in the Bible where it said "and God laughed." It occurred to him, as he fumbled the washcloth in a vain attempt to cover himself, that this might actually be Satan, attempting to trick him.

"C'mon, Dougie," the Voice said, "You've been my faithful servant for how many years now, but you still find it easier to believe in Lucifer than me?"

"No, sir," Doug stammered, spinning the shower knob to the

'Off" position and clambering awkwardly out of the tub. "I mean, Lord - it's just that, well, I, uh -"

"I know, I *know*," the Voice sighed. "You think you're insane because you can actually hear me - happens all the time."

"All the <u>time?</u>" Doug said curiously, wondering how many people actually had this experience on a daily basis.

"Well, a *lot*," the Voice amended. "But that's not important right now. We need to talk about Edna."

Despite himself, a groan escaped Doug. Edna Becker owned the property adjacent to the church cemetery, a huge, shabby Victorian home that reminded Doug uncomfortably of the Addams family cartoon. A more cantankerous, argumentative old biddy Doug had never met. He had not, in fact *met* Edna, but her continuous phone calls to the manse about this or that perceived annoyance had driven Frances the church secretary, and Lillian, Doug's wife, to the brink of mayhem.

"I understand," the Voice said. "She's a piece of work, but that *is* your calling, son. Besides, you've had it pretty easy for the past few years, decent sized parish, not too many scandals in the congregation - time for a little challenge!"

"I suppose you're right, Lord," Doug said. "It's just that she seems so unreachable."

"Considering the fact that you always let Frances or Lillian handle her, I doubt that you're in much of a position to judge, Dougie," the Voice said. No one had called Douglas "Dougie" since his Aunt Alberta died when Doug was 40, and it made him feel strangely small.

"I know she's difficult," the Voice said, "but she needs someone to pay some attention to her, make her feel connected to life again, and you're the man."

"If you say so, Lord," Doug said. "What do you want me to do, exactly?"

"Doug?" Lillian's musical voice came from the other side of the bathroom door. "Did you want something, dear?"

"NO! Uh, no, Lillian, that's ok - just practicing my sermon," Doug said loudly. "I'll be out in a second." Doug scrambled for his shorts and wrestled them on over still-damp legs.

"Well . . . all right, then," Lillian's voice sounded puzzled, but after a moment Doug heard her footsteps receding down the upstairs hallway.

When Doug and Lillian arrived in Linden three years ago, he had been warned by more than one of the parishoners that Edna was somewhat eccentric and that he'd best just let her be, but Doug was full of the zeal of the Lord, and as soon as they'd settled into the parsonage he'd trotted across the lawn, cut through the cemetery and bounded up the steps onto Edna's front porch, hoping for at least a civil welcome.

What he'd gotten was nothing. After ringing the bell, which had a dangerous short that gave him quite a shock when he touched it, Doug waited for a very long time, but no one came to the door. Turning to go, he'd caught a quick movement out of the corner of his eye as the draperies at the front bay window were twitched back into place, and he half considered ringing one more time, but thought better of it.

"Just as well," said Olly Johnson, one of the church elders who ran the TrueTest Hardware store on Central Avenue told Doug. "Woman could eat railroad spikes for breakfast and spit nails for lunch. Surprised she didn't electrocute you with that dadblasted doorbell of hers." He glanced at Doug slyly. "Us locals know enough to knock if we go over there for somethin'. Course, she doesn't always answer the door then, either."

Doug had decided to let things be after that, and was grateful to have Frances and Lillian handle her frequent complaints, but apparently the Lord had more involvement in mind.

"So, let's say Friday," the Voice said. "Friday would be a good time to visit. Oh, and Douglas?"

"Yes, Lord?"

"I've seen everything about you naked, even your soul, so being embarrassed is rather redundant, although, you could use a little work around the middle. Too much of Lillian's home cooking."

The Voice was silent for the remainder of the week, but Doug found it impossible to forget the conversation. He vacillated between thinking perhaps he was going round the bend mentally, and feeling oddly special, as though he had been chosen for some tremendous blessing. Friday morning, his sermon pretty much wrapped up except for a few touches, Doug steeled himself and crossed the cemetery, stepping carefully up the broad, cracked front steps of Edna's porch. Taking a deep breath, he rapped at the door just to the right of the grimy glass panel. The house, built in what Doug thought must have been somewhere around the mid 1920's, had leaded glass windows, a broad, welcoming porch, and the look of a home that was once well-loved. Now, everything about it bespoke neglect.

When it seemed that no one was about to respond, Doug raised his fist for a second try when suddenly the door was wrenched open and a rheumy, red-rimmed blue eye peered at him through the two-inch aperture.

"Well, what is it?" the eye's owner snapped in a voice like a rusty hinge.

"Miss Becker?" Doug said politely. "I'm Reverend Douglas Car-"

"I know who you are," the voice responded. "The question is, what do you want, banging at my door like some salesman? And be quick about it - the last thing I need is to catch a chill."

Well," Doug began . . . what was he doing here, really? He

couldn't very well tell the woman God had sent him - it would sound too Baptist, and besides, he got a strong feeling that she was waiting for an excuse to slam the door in his face, and that just might do the trick.

". . . . I was just wondering," Doug said. "That is, we've never actually met, and I always like to get to know our neighbors, see if there is anything I can do to help them out, establish a cordial relationship."

"So, where were you the last two summers, then, when that wretched Carter boy insisted on mowing the cemetery grass at the ungodly hour of 6:00 am every Saturday morning?" Edna Becker said, but Doug noticed that she opened the door a few more inches.

"I am sorry about that, Miss Becker," Doug said in what he hoped was a suitably remorseful tone.

"Balderdash!" the woman snorted. "I don't have the time or the stamina to stand here in a draft and listen to you prattle on. If you're going to keep talking, then come in and do it like a civilized person."

She turned away abruptly and Doug stepped through the door into what seemed to be another era. Directly ahead to his left lay what had once been a grand staircase, and Doug's gaze followed the lines of the curved oak bannister that rose fluidly upward toward a round stained glass window that bathed the landing at the top in a rainbow of color.

"Well, don't just stand there gaping," Edna said sternly. "My mother always entertained guests in the parlor - come this way."

The fireplace hadn't been used, or cleaned, in years, Doug guessed, and the portrait over the mantel bore a fine patina of dust. Edna motioned him to a blanket-draped chair, and seated herself across from him. She was a small woman, no taller than perhaps 5 feet, with a fleece of soft white hair drawn into a loose knot at the nape of her neck, and she looked frail to Doug, a fine network of blue veins visible beneath her translucent skin, a pronounced tremor in her decidedly arthritic hands.

"Sit" Edna commanded. Doug sat. If there had been any time when Doug needed the Lord to intervene, this was it, but no message seemed forthcoming. He realized suddenly that he had been sitting on the rump-sprung easy chair with his head cocked upward and to the right in an attitude of listening, and Edna was staring at him as if he were completely out of his mind.

"Miss Becker," Doug began carefully, "I truly am sorry about the mowing- Simon has summer school classes, and he -"

"I don't need to hear excuses, young man," Edna barked. "Don't care about them. My father always said, 'Sorries are for the people who say them.' What I need is to be able to sleep peacefully on Saturday morning."

Doug cringed inwardly. This was going to be a lot harder than he'd thought. "I'd be glad to see what I can do for you Edna - may I call you Edna? Actually, I wanted to invite you to services at Good Shepherd if you'd like to -"

"You may call me Miss Becker," Edna said sharply. "That's what's wrong with the world nowadays - no respect. As for visiting your church, Reverend, I get enough aggravation from that boy and his lawnmower and those infernal bells bonging away on Sunday mornings. What I'd like is to have civil neighbors, and to be left alone. I have no use for church, nor for the social rituals that take place there. Your God, if He does, indeed exist, has left me to my own devices for seventy-eight years, and I've done likewise. Now, if that was all you came for I'll thank you to take yourself back home and minister to someone who needs it. You can let yourself out."

Numbly Doug got to his feet. That, he supposed, was that. Still, just walking out on the old harridan wasn't the Christian thing to do. At the doorway, he paused, turned back toward the parlor.

"Miss Becker," Doug said, "I will speak to Simon about the mowing, but I hope you'll not be offended if I come by now and then, just to be neighborly."

There was a moment of silence.

"If you're coming as a neighbor and not to proselytize." Edna said grudgingly. "Just make sure you've got something worthwhile to say."

"Goodbye, then," Doug said, closing the door softly behind him.

"Nice job," the Voice said suddenly as Doug skirted the Williams family plot in the center of the church cemetery. He started, bashing his left hip painfully into a large tombstone. "Tough nut to crack, isn't she?"

"Yes, sir," Doug said, glancing quickly around to see if anyone could hear. "I wasn't sure what you wanted me to do. I mean, she doesn't seem at all receptive. It almost sounds as though she doesn't really *believe* in You."

"It happens sometimes," the Voice said calmly. "Sooner or later most of you come around. The important thing is that I believe in you, so don't worry about it. You did just what I wanted, you opened up a line of communication."

Doug thought to himself that as uncivil as the old lady was, referring to the dialogue they'd had as communication was a huge exaggeration.

"That might be true, Doug" the Voice said, "but it's my job to love the unlovable, and since you're representing me -"

Doug stopped suddenly. "You can hear me *think*?"

"Of course," the Voice replied. "Why do you think it says in my Book "Be still and *know*?" If everybody I talk to walked around carrying on a conversation with Me out loud, do you know how many of you would be hospitalized for lunacy? A lot more than there are now, that's for sure."

"So, all those people in psychiatric facilities - DO you talk to them?" Doug asked.

God sounded amused. "Some of them, but there's usually something else wrong with them already. You know, you can be crazy and still hear Me. I don't discriminate."

Less than reassured by the Lord's explanation, Doug closed the cemetery gate quietly behind him and crossed the lawn to the parsonage back door.

"Shoes off, please," Lillian sang out as he stepped into the back hallway. "I just mopped this floor, not that one would notice. The rummage sale committee is coming over tonight, and I'd like them to think I occasionally clean around here. How did it go?"

The parsonage, built in the early 50's, was a neat Cape Cod - serviceable, but small. When Doug, Lillian and the three kids ended up in the kitchen at the same time, there was barely room to turn around. Still, Doug was grateful to have a parish as solid as Good Shepherd.

"Well - OK, I guess," Doug said. "She wasn't exactly cordial, but I did manage to talk to her, which is what the Lord told me to do, so . . ." Doug noticed that Lillian was staring at him strangely. "I mean, where I was led . . . lost sheep and all . . . ." He trailed off.

"I'm surprised she didn't read you the riot act from behind the front door," Lillian said, turning to the sink. Doug heaved an inward sigh of relief and headed for his study.

Over the next days, Doug found himself thinking about Edna Becker far more than he would have liked to. Seated at his desk in the church office, he would find his gaze wandering to the house across the cemetery, wondering what it must be like to live alone at Edna's age, her family gone, no friends to visit. On the following Friday morning, his sermon bogged down in mid-stride, and although Doug asked for help the Lord was conspicuously silent. Without quite knowing why, Doug found himself on Edna's doorstep, his rough draft clutched in a hand which, he noticed as he waited for Edna to answer the door, was beginning to sweat in anticipation.

The door creaked open suddenly.

"Well, what is it?" Edna said tersely. Doug attempted to compose himself.

"I just wanted to let you know I've talked to Simon, and we've agreed that he'll try to mow after his class on Saturday. That way -"

"Fine." The door began to close.

"And . . . and, well," Doug said, "I was just wondering if you might have a minute - you see, I'm working on something that's rather problematic, and I thought -"

There was a momentary silence, then Edna opened the door, grudgingly.

"Whatever it is, I'm sure you don't need *my* assistance. Ah, well, come in, then, if you're coming."

Doug seated himself on the lumpy parlor chair and waited while Edna settled in across from him.

"What is it? I hope you're not thinking of asking me to donate to one of your worthy causes, mission field work or ladies' guild, or whatever they're doing over there these days," Edna snapped.

"Oh, no, nothing like that." Doug said. He wondered why it was this woman had the power to reduce him to a nervous 7-year old shuddering in the principal's office over some imagined infraction. "I've hit a sticky spot in my sermon for this week. I understand that you are a writer, so I thought perhaps you might be willing to share the benefit of your experience with me."

Douglas had gleaned this bit of information from Vernon Harp, the barber, as he was getting his bi-monthly trim. What

Vernon had said was that Edna had written the local history and social engagement calendars for the Herald for many years. She had, as Vernon recalled, a flair for it, and it seemed a pity she'd never done much else in the way of writing.

"Ah. I see." Edna said. Doug thought he detected the slightest hint of pleasure in her tone, so he pushed on resolutely.

"I'm trying to explain that we should try to care for others the way the Lord cares for us," Doug said. "It's for the beginner's Sunday school class, and I -"

"Well, I fervently hope you're not planning on using that tired old shepherd and his sheep analogy," Edna snorted. "*Sheep*, of all things! Have you ever actually observed sheep? Stupid creatures, constantly milling around waiting for someone to herd them somewhere. I don't presume to know what your preference might be, but I, for one, would find it highly offensive to be compared to a farm animal, particularly one with not a lick of common sense."

That was exactly the imagery Doug had been going to use, and he found himself rather put out at Edna's criticism. He really didn't need help, but it seemed a subtle way of making contact, and perhaps ingratiating himself.

"What would you suggest?"

"Simplicity," Edna replied. "Children like things simple, uncomplicated. You mustn't be condescending, mind you, but you need to be clear. You're a parent, aren't you?"

"Yes . . . yes, I am," Doug said. Then, "Oh. Well, of course! How could I have missed it - we care for our children the way God cares for us. Perfect! I should have thought of that."

"Indeed you should, instead of bothering me with it," Edna said. "It's very trite, of course, but then religion tends to be. Was there anything else?"

"Ask about the pictures," the Voice said directly into Doug's right ear.

"What pictures?" Doug blurted. Edna flinched.

"I beg your pardon?"

"What wonderful pictures! Around the room," Doug gestured nervously. "Who are they all, if you don't mind my asking?"

Edna turned stiffly in her chair to nod at the portrait over the long-unused fireplace. "That is my mother, Eleanora Weisman Becker. My father had it painted the year after they were married, shortly before my mother learned she was carrying my brother Milton. To the left there, that is my father, Martin Becker. The pocket watch he is holding belonged to my great grandfather Theodore, and next to father is Milton, and next over is Theodore the second - we called him Teddy. On the right is my sister Francine, and next to her Lucille and Grace, they were born eleven months apart, and that is myself on the end."

She gestured to the west wall.

"There are great-grandfather Theodore and Great-grandmother Elvira, and Grandfather Demson. That's grandmother Sylvia seated in the single photograph; she died when father was born, and there was never a chance for them to have a formal portrait painted together. Most unfortunate - they say grandfather never quite got over the shock. When I knew him he was a stern, taciturn man, dignified but without emotion."

"And that one?" Doug asked.

It was a small, modestly framed photograph of a young man, taken out of doors and unposed. He was not a particularly handsome man, his white shirt was rumpled and open at the neck, his hair windblown, but there was kindness in his eyes, and he had a smile that drew one's eye back to the picture for a second look, a pure, sweet smile borne of genuine goodness.

Edna faced the photograph, and there was a momentary silence so deep and profound that Douglas found himself holding his breath.

"That," Edna said in a voice gone suddenly young, "is Winston Hale."

"Winston was a junior accountant in my father's office. He came here straight from the University of Michigan. His family was from out East, Camden, Massachusetts, his father had a law firm there, but Winston wanted to be his own man, he said, make something of himself without riding on his family's reputation. He was a very independent person, a person of character."

Doug turned to look at Edna, but her eyes were fastened on the photograph.

"My father said when he first met Winston he thought he'd never known a young man with such presence. Mind you, Father was not easily impressed - he was quite demanding of all of us, although Mother simply had to raise an eyebrow and he would soften. Still, he was truly fond of Winston from the very beginning. We all were. Teddy and Winston were close in age, and like two peas in a pod, always kidding about with one another. When Teddy realized that Winston was . . . " Edna faltered, a flush creeping into her sallow cheeks. "Well, after Winston let him know what his intentions were toward me, Teddy teased us both relentlessly."

Douglas made a soft, listening sort of murmur.

"Winston loved to laugh," Edna said. "He found joy in the simplest small things like flying a kite or helping Grace catch frogs. She was a tomboy, loved being with Winston because he always talked Teddy into letting her go fishing with them, or to the park. He had this huge, wonderful laugh that would simply burst from him when you least expected it, like the sun coming out from behind a cloud.

Oh, he was serious about his career, of course, intensely so. Father said he was the kind of man who could have run the firm someday." She was still.

When he could no longer stand the silence, Doug cleared his throat. Edna blinked, turned to look at Douglas, a long, measuring stare.

"I have not spoken of this in more than thirty years," she said finally. "Winston went back East for his eldest sister's wedding. He had wanted me to go, but we weren't actually engaged yet, not formally. Back then there was etiquette to follow, not like things are nowadays. It wouldn't have been acceptable for me to travel alone with a single man, and I'd only met his family once when they came for a visit.

There were several parties planned for the week leading up to the wedding. One of them was a boating excursion on the lake at the family summer home. Somehow the boat got hung up in some weeds, and Winston was a great swimmer, so of course he volunteered to dive down and see what was the matter.

"He never came up."

Edna turned a little away from Douglas to stare, unseeing out the living room window.

"I'm so sorry, Miss Becker," Douglas said finally.

She turned, fixing him with a cool stare.

"Indeed," Edna said. Her voice was flat. "At least you've the courtesy to spare me the usual litany of excuses for the Deity's actions. I have heard them all, I assure you, and they would be no more a comfort to me now than they were then."

Douglas nodded. "Sometimes His ways are a mystery even to me," he began, but Edna cut him off sharply.

"If, indeed, there is a God, I should have no more concern for Him than He has shown for me." She gazed down at her clenched hands.

"I will not deny that my life has been one of privilege. I have wanted for little, and my father saw to it that I would always be cared for, as he did for all of us; but losing Winston was the universe's cruelest joke. If I had been meant to suffer, then my life could not have been more exquisitely designed, for this house, these extravagances around me simply serve to remind me every day of the one thing I have lost."

Doug was well acquainted with grief. He sat wisely in silence for what seemed an interminable amount of time until Edna regained her composure and raised her eyes to his.

"I trust that you will be gentleman enough not to repeat what I have told you, nor do I wish to speak of it ever again," she said, straightening her shoulders.

"You have my word, Miss Becker," Doug rose, feeling distinctly that he was being dismissed. " Lillian is making pumpkin muffins for the church rummage this weekend, and I'd like to bring you some to express my gratitude for your help with the sermon, if it's all right."

"That is kind of you, but not necessary," Edna said.

Then, just as Douglas reached the front door she spoke again. "Reverend?"

"Yes ma'am?"

"There is one thing you might do for me. You might inquire if there is a good, dependable handyman who will work for a reasonable wage. My doorbell has been out of order for quite some time now. I think perhaps it is time to have it fixed."

Angel

Mr. Leo left tonight at 2:56 AM. I've gotten into the habit of noting the time like the nurses and doctors do. I almost missed it - I was tired, and it was so gentle, he was holding my hand, then he was gone. He was so looking forward to seeing his Emma, he told me, and from the little half-smile on his lips, maybe she made it on time, although he said once, chuckling, that she would probably be late like always.

Relationships are short here. I only knew Mr. Leo for six days, and mostly we talked about his life, but I knew everything that counted about him, even things that he had kept secret from Emma, like the girl in Germany he slept with when he was in the Army. The day before he stopped talking, he struggled to sit up a little on the pillow and looked at me sharply.

"What about you, missy?" he asked. "You have secrets, don't you?"

I just smiled and asked if he'd like some water, and we moved on to other things. He was a sweet old man, and I'll miss him, at least for a while.

It was raining the night they brought me here to the ER. I was 14, and I hadn't slept in two days. My arm was broken, my lip cut, a lot of bruises, and I hurt inside, under my ribs where Jason kicked me They kept asking me my name, but I I just said

I couldn't remember what happened, which wasn't true, but I wasn't going back into foster care for anything. The nurses were so kind to me, gave me something for pain, and were really gentle, even when they took me to Xray. I could tell they'd probably seen girls like me too often. I was in and out, so tired, and after all the tests they gave me a bed in a room where it was clean and quiet, There was something about that room, the peace in it, that made me feel safe for the first time in what seemed like forever. One of the nurses came in, held my hand and stayed till I went to sleep.

The soft voices, the muted noise from the machines, the dim lights at night always make me happy. It's as if life is in slow motion most of the time – it's why I decided to stay.

This hospital is one of the largest in the whole country. People are always getting lost, even with the colored lines they have on the floors to tell you where to go. When I was on the floor days I would see people standing in a corridor with this bewildered look. It's confusing, I know, it took me a year or so to find places to sleep, places where I could be invisible.

The best about being here is that I have friends.

Not the staff - everyone has a badge with a name, and that's important to them. They want ask questions about why you are on that floor, if you're visiting someone. Of course, it's their job, but I know how things work. When I was on the street I would sometimes pretend to be shopping in a store just to get in from the cold, and the first thing they would ask was your name, if you were with anyone, and if you didn't answer they made you leave. The maintenance staff is nice, they just want to get their work done and go home, but the patients, like Mr. Leo, are my friends. When you are really sick, all the phoniness falls away. You just want to be seen, listened to, comforted, and even though I felt useless when I came here, paid attention, and finally figured out this - I am good at helping people who are sick, and good at helping people die.

There's so much to learn here. You have to move from one floor to another, don't stay in any one place for too long, you really need to blend in, I figured out that there are some areas where it's easier, but some of them are just places I don't want to be. The ER is usually crazy, people everywhere, chaos on weekends, but it's also the worst, the saddest. My first week here, they brought in a boy, not much older than me, blood all over him. His friends just left him lying in front of the doors and drove off, and he was hurt really bad. A whole bunch of staff came running, and they were paging for help. I couldn't see what was happening, but I could hear him at first, calling for his Mama, over and over, and then it stopped. Later, when everybody left, I peeked around the curtain. They'd cleaned him up so his family wouldn't see all the blood, but he looked so small, so alone that it reminded me how alone I was. I still don't like to go there.

I did have a friend on the staff once, not too long after I came. She worked nights on the third floor, a tiny little lady from Mexico. Birdie caught me sleeping in a storage closet. Usually I can hear the cleaning carts, but Birdie was always extra quiet, careful not to wake the patients. I woke up, startled with her bending over me, her brown eyes just a few inches from mine.

"Oh, sorry," I stammered, flustered. "Guess I dozed off."

"Hush, Mija," she said, putting her finger to her lips. "Is ok, you look tired. Did you eat today?"

I just stared at her, afraid because she knew I didn't belong.

"Here, I got banana," she said, rummaging in a brown bag on her cart. "You gotta eat."

"No, that's ok," I told her. I got a sandwich a while ago. Thank you, though."

"I see you here and there," she said. "Maybe you stay, no place for you to go? OK, not so bad place."

She patted me on the arm. I nodded - it was hard, nobody knowing me - even on the street you had people who knew you, not friends, just people.

"I stay quiet, sometimes I see things," she said. "I see you, you sit with patients, listen, make feel better so they no cry at night. Night is sometimes hard," Birdie said. "You do good . When you come here?"

I never talked to anybody on the staff, knew from being on the street how to be invisible, but Birdie was different. There was kindness in her eyes, and I needed that so much. I started talking, told her how I got there, how I never knew my dad, mom drank too much at night, about the foster homes and how I finally ended up on the street. It seemed like I couldn't shut up, I even told her about Jason, how he was so nice to me at first, bought me food, told me how pretty I was, and what happened later with the men.

Birdie just listened, but she cried a little when I got to the awful part, how I ended up here.

"Ah, Mija, I am so sorry," she said, wiping her eyes. "It's gonna be ok now, you gonna be ok, I know this. I am gonna pray for you tonight, every night. You will see."

I loved Birdie, and I know she loved me, too. Sometimes she would find me on her breaks, and we would just talk about our lives. Sometimes I would pretend to myself that Birdie was my real mother, the one I wished I had.

When Birdie retired she promised to come back to see me, and she did for a while, but the visits got further and further apart. Every time I saw her she seemed smaller, her hair turning silver, her walk slower. She talked about going back to Mexico, and maybe that's what she did. It's been a really long time since I've seen her, not sure how long, but I miss her every day.

Time folds in on itself here. I used to pay attention to the TV, what day it was, what year, but night time it is easier for me to be out and about, so I don't pay attention to that stuff anymore. I spend time with people, but it's the ones who are alone in their rooms, who are sleeping, or who are floating in that space between here and There.

It took me a while, but now when people are getting ready to go, I can sense it, sometimes even hear it. I'll walk past a room – I call it 'walking rounds,' like the rounds the doctors do – and something calls me there. Sometimes it's the smell of a wedding bouquet that someone is remembering, a snatch of an old song, but a lot of the time it's just a feeling.

If there are other people in the room, I just move on. Sometimes, a patient wants to be alone. I didn't understand that at first, but one old lady, Helen, explained it to me. She was ninety, all her family gone but for a son in San Francisco who she hadn't seen in years. I sat with her sometimes while she was waiting, mostly just to be there for her, but that night she told me to go.

"Honey, it's like life is a big, wonderful party. You've had so much fun, and it's getting late and you're tired, but people keep wanting you to stay, so you do, even though you just want to go home to your bed. It's so much easier to just slip away while everyone else is still enjoying themselves. You see?"

I nodded.

"Good." She patted my hand. "Now, you go on, sweetie. I'm going to go home."

I never finished high school, so I don't guess I'm very smart, but it makes me feel good to help with kids when they get scared at night, maybe because I remember what it was like to be scared, and I'm really good at just listening to people, which is sometimes all they need.

I've been sitting with Carrie for almost two weeks. She has

leukemia, and I can tell she's afraid. Her mom and Dad don't want to tell her how sick she is so they just pretend everything is going to be OK, even though Carrie knows better. We talk about school, how she never really had a boyfriend, the things she misses and tonight she asked me what was going to happen to her, so I told her what I knew. Sometimes someone you love, or who loves you, comes to get you when it's time, sometimes even a dog or cat. Sometimes there's music that is so beautiful you want to listen forever, and sometimes there's just a warm, bright light that makes you want to get closer to it. I held Carrie's hand till she went to sleep, and then I came up to the roof. It's really hot this summer, and I just need to breathe for a bit and see the stars.

Later some of the staff comes out on the other side of the roof where the smokers go, gossiping like everybody does. I can tell one of them is Gwen, one of Carrie's nurses her voice with a soft, Jamaican lilt. I don't pay much attention at first, but then I hear Gwen say that one of her patients is 'on the way out.'

"She said the oddest thing to me tonight," Gwen said, "she told me an angel visited her and she isn't so afraid anymore."

"Yeah, heard that before, more than once." Another voice, one of the older nurses, slightly familiar.

"Me, too." A guy's voice. "I've only been here three weeks, but that's kind of a legend around here, isn't it? Weird, pretty much the same story from everybody, she comes at night, stays with them till they fall asleep. Creeps me out."

"Not really," the older nurse. "I think it's a gift. We can't be with everybody, and it would be nice to know they had someone there with them when they go."

"I haven't lost anybody yet."

Gwen. "That first one is tough."

Older nurse again, I think her name is Sara. "I still remember mine, over twenty years ago. Was my second week here and they brought in this girl, found her in an alley, beaten so badly, barely conscious. A sweet little thing, young. It was slow that night, so we put her in a room and I sat with her while we waited for someone from Social Services to come, held her hand. Her hand was so small, and she had this tiny birthmark on the inside of her left wrist. There were some internal injuries, thought she would be ok, but I had to step out for a minute and she just . . .stopped breathing."

They are all quiet.

I look at the stars for a while longer, thinking about all the friends who have gone, some like Mr. Leo, here for just a few days, some like Carrie, who I've known longer. I'm really going to miss her, but someone else will come along.

I look down at my wrist, at the brown oval that my mom used to tell me was where she spilled a drop of coffee on me when I was a baby.

On the way back downstairs I stop by Carrie's door just to check if she's still waiting. She's awake, waves to me to come in.

"Can you stay a little?" she asks me. Her voice is fading, that wispy softness that comes when people are close to the in between place.

"Sure."

"Thanks," she murmurs to me, reaches for my arm. "Friends. So nice to me. Don't even know your name."

"That's OK," I tell her. "It doesn't matter, really."

"If you want you can call me Angel."

A Dog to Beware Of

I COULD HAVE BEEN AN ACTRESS, YOU KNOW. MOTHER ALWAYS said so, even when I was six and played the Snowflake Queen in the first grade Christmas Pageant. I was the only freshman at Prentice Junior College to ever land the lead in the drama department's annual production - I was Blanche in 'Streetcar'- and even though Mother felt the role was too sophisticated for me, she was proud of my performance.

Mother wasn't sure I should be going on the Spring break trip, especially not to New Orleans.

"So decadent," she said, pursing her lips. "You know, Lilith, things can happen to a girl in a place like that." Still, the school promised that we would be properly chaperoned, so Mother grudgingly gave her consent.

No sense dwelling on the past, I always say, but I sometimes do wonder what might have been had I not met Ferris. Anyway, there I was, strolling by myself through the French Quarter, totally enchanted. I'd never been anywhere on my own before, and Jefferson Square with its artists strewn along the streets seemed as magical as Paris. The other girls had stopped at the grocery for muffaletta sandwiches, but I decided to be brave and look for someplace to get a cup of coffee. I had a fine figure back then, and a girl needs to watch her figure, you know, especially if she wants to pursue a career in the public eye.

I found a lovely little cafe just across the way from the Farmers' Market, and ordered a coffee with milk, partly as an indulgence but mostly because I'd never drunk coffee all that much, and the bitterness was hard to get used to. There was music coming from somewhere nearby, and I didn't pay much attention at first, but after I sat down at one of those little round tables I started looking around. That's when I first laid eyes on Ferris.

He was sitting on the corner of a brick retaining wall singing, a broad-shouldered young man clutching his guitar with a kind of fierce intensity, his head cocked to one side, a single lock of wavy hair dangling down over his forehead. The rest of his hair was gleaming, jet-black, but that single, wild lock was silver white, and every now and then, between chords, he'd reach up and push it back, even though it wouldn't stay.

Ferris never was much of a singer, truth be told. He had a fine speaking voice - smooth and soft, cultured - but it was more the words he used, the way he put things. He was singing a blues song, rough chords that barely meshed with the lyrics.

"I was a man of means, with a woman gave me fine love,
Now I'm turned-out and turned-down, just a dog to beware of
Lord, ain't it a long, hard life?"

He looked up then, looked around, and his eyes caught mine. I swear I felt the heat rising up my neck till I thought I'd melt right there, and I looked down at my cup real quick. Still, when I looked up again, he was still staring, with big, blue-green eyes, eyes a color I'd never seen in nature before.

I know it sounds vain, but I was an attractive young woman then. My hair was very blonde - Mother used to call me her "butter baby" because my hair was so truly yellow - and I was blessed with fine features, generous lips and a straight, perfect nose. Even so, I'd never been stared at by a man that way, and I didn't know whether to stare back, or to bolt and run.

A minute later I had no choice. He finished the song, put his guitar carefully in its' case, and made a beeline for my table.

"Allow me to introduce myself," he said, bending and offering me his hand. "My name is Ferris Markham, a minstrel of modest means and a native of our fair city. Would you be so kind as to allow me the pleasure of your company for a brief while?"

"Well, I was just about to go, you see, I'm to meet my friends," I replied, trying to sound nonchalant, as though strange men regularly accosted me on the street.

"Ah, but you must finish your coffee, Cher," Ferris nodded toward my cup. "I was about to have a cup myself. Surely you can spare a few minutes. Let me get some, and I'll join you."

I just sat there, helpless, and a minute or so later he was back, pulling up a chair from the next table and settling himself on it with a sigh. He spooned three or four huge spoons of sugar into his coffee, took a long sip of his and leaned forward, peering into my cup.

"Is that milk I see in dere ?" he asked, glancing up at me with those amazing eyes through a thicket of black lashes. "As I suspected, you are not yet acquainted with our custom."

"What custom is that?" I asked warily.

He smiled, leaning back in his chair, putting his hands behind his head. "There's only one way to drink coffee in N'awlins, Cher," he said. "Black as hell, strong as death, and sweet as love."

I had been smitten by his looks, but I believe that moment was the moment I fell hopelessly in love. Of course, the line was not original - few of his lines ever were - but that was long before I knew that Ferris' accent had been acquired by months of careful listening and practice, and that the minstrel of the Vieux Carre was, in actuality, Earl Watson formerly of Rollo, Missouri - so I was enchanted.

We sat there for Lord knows how long, and Ferris finally convinced me to meet him at the Cafe du Monde later that night, after the other girls had gone to sleep. He would show me the real Quarter, he said, and indeed he did. We had beignets and coffee, and we walked till two in the morning, talking.

Ferris explained to me that he had a small inheritance which allowed him to pursue his musical career. It was small, all right - one hundred and forty-two dollars a month, and some rooms on the upper floor of a real estate office on Carondelet, between Perdido and Union. "Here we are, dahlin'," he said grandly the first time I went up to his place. "I call this humble dwelling Maison J'espere." Maison Despair is more like it, but back then I was too blinded by romance to notice how tiny the rooms were, and how shabby everything was.

Isn't it odd how time passes so quickly? I can remember those first days, even those first few years, as clearly as though a play were unfolding in front of me. By the end of the week, I knew I couldn't possibly leave Ferris. Of course, Mother had a fit when I called her. You wouldn't believe the awful things she said to me, once she realized I truly wouldn't change my mind. Ferris, to his credit, was dear about the whole thing. "Listen, dahlin'," he said as I sat weeping against his shoulder, "this is doubtless an awful shock for your poor mother. It's not good to burn bridges, you know - perhaps you should go back for a few days, gather your things, try to talk some sense into your Mamaw."

"No," I wailed. "I just want to be with YOU!"

"There, there, sugar," he said, patting me gently. "Nevah you mind."

Ferris always was a gentle man. I don't ever recall him raising his voice to me in all the years we were together. Even when I'd get upset and frustrated over something, he'd just say "There, there, sugar, don't carry on so," and make me even madder. Still, in those days, I felt he was my rock.

We married at the justice of the peace. Nothing fancy, just a simple gold band I helped pay for, some flowers Ferris picked for me and I wore one of my travelling dresses, the soft lawn one. We settled into his rooms as nice as you please. During the day I'd tidy up around the place, and after a few disasters in the kitchen, Mrs. Kelson from across the street took pity on Ferris and invited me into her kitchen for lessons. I became a superb cook, if I may say so. I'd put a pot of gumbo or dirty rice on the stove and Ferris would come home most nights with a bag of beignets, some caramel sugar buns from the bakery, perhaps some chocolates. "A little lagniappe, dahlin,'" he'd say. I never had much of a sweet tooth, but Ferris dearly appreciated dessert, so we always had sweets in the house for after dinner. Ferris loved to eat. "A sen-sue-all experience, Lily," he'd say, pushing his chair back and loosening his belt. "You do know how to satisfy a man - in many ways." He'd stare meaningfully at me across the table, and I'd blush like everything.

Ferris never actually suggested that I get work, but after awhile it became clear that we needed the extra income - musicians don't make much, you know, unless they're quite famous, and Ferris was struggling. When I got the job waiting tables at Broussard's, Ferris was simply delighted. "That's my girl, Cher," he said, dancing me around the living room. "Now we will be able to improve our lot, so t'speak."

The job itself was not a picnic, but I was young, and my natural acting ability was a great help to me. I often thought of myself as onstage in a sort of improvisational roll - the scene changed and the characters were different at each table, and I had to adapt accordingly. In fact, I drew quite generous tips, perhaps as much for my appearance as for my performance. I dreamed that someday a real producer would come along and catch my act, tell me that a girl with my style was just what they were looking for, and fly me off to Hollywood - with Ferris, of course.

When I worked day shift, I'd change into my own clothes in the little locker room at Broussards and walk over to meet Ferris. Sometimes he'd be doing well, so I'd just get a cup of coffee and sit and listen to him play for a while. When he finished, we'd go stroll around the Quarter. There was a lovely little antique shop on Royal, lots of finely polished English and French furniture - and Ferris used to promise me that someday I'd have a houseful of antiques. The proprietor, Mr. Chenault, was always sitting outside with Maximillian, his French bulldog, and Ferris never failed to bring some tidbit for him.

"Lookit dere, Cher," he'd chuckle as we turned onto Royal. "That's one fine dog." Max would leap to his feet as soon as he saw us, dancing from one foot to the other, his buggy little eyes just about whirling in his head with delight, snorting like he was about to expire. Ferris would squat down and rub his head while I exchanged pleasantries with Mr. Chenault, and I swear Ferris and Max would have their own conversation.

It was actually Mr. Chenault who gave me the idea to give Ferris the puppy for his birthday. We ran into each other on the street one afternoon while I was on my way to meet Ferris.

"Miss Lily," Mr. Chenault said, tipping his hat. "Where might Mr. Ferris be?"

I'm on my way to meet him just now," I said, bending to pat Max on the head.

Mr. Chenault smiled beatifically down at Max. "Mr. Ferris surely does love that dog," he said. "Not too many folk can appreciate what a fine dog these animals are, but Mr. Ferris, he has an eye for dogflesh. He should have one of his own."

The more I thought, the better an idea it seemed. I started saving my tips, stashing them in a little jar at the back of the closet, and Mr. Chenault found me a breeder that was willing to sell me a puppy for a reasonable price, as long as I promised not to breed it or use it for show.

I wish you could have seen the look on Ferris' face when I walked into the salon with that puppy. It was the ugliest little thing I ever saw, with a tiny pea-head and huge bat-ears, its nose all pushed in, but Ferris took one look at him and fell in love.

"Aw, Cher!" Ferris said, scooping the puppy out of my arms. "He's so fine!" The puppy wiggled around and started washing Ferris' face, wetting all down the front of his shirt from excitement. Ferris didn't even mind.

"Poor little polliwog," he said, rubbing the puppy behind the ears. "In't he somthin, Lily?"

"What are you going to name him?" I asked.

"Ah, THAT I already know," Ferris said, settling down in his big easy chair with the puppy wiggling on his chest. "He needs the name of an artist, somebody with talent, a maestro. I'm going to call him Poochini."

I shook my head at the silliness of it, but then I expect Ferris had a right to call him whatever he wanted. I hoped that it would be his companion while I was at work, and indeed he was. The fact is, I believe Ferris loved that little dog more than he ever loved me. They went everywhere together, and folk at the cafes and restaurants began to save tidbits for Poochini. "A leetl somtin' for the dawg," they'd say, waving Ferris across the street. He taught Poochini to shake hands 'Thank you,' an' it wasn't long before he got so wide he waddled. When I mentioned it to Ferris, he just laughed and patted his own belly. "Takin' after his Papa, Cher," he said.

I just smiled, but as time went on, Ferris and that dog did

begin to look more and more alike. All those cups of coffee loaded with sugar, sweets from the bakery, a bite here, a bite there, all added up. The first time I had to let out Ferris' pants, he we chuckled over it. "Guess I'm on the way to bein' a success, Lily," he said, "a man of substance, so to speak." Unfortunately, his waist kept getting larger and larger, but the same couldn't be said for our income.

It seems as though the last few years, my whole life was consumed by food. I'd go to work, serve platefuls of the richest, heaviest dishes you can imagine, dripping with bearnaise sauce, butter, cream - then I'd go home and Ferris would be wanting dinner. Oh, I tried cooking sparingly - broiled fish, a lean cut of beef - but Ferris was so disappointed, I could see it in his eyes. "This is like no food a-tall, dahlin'," he'd say . "No flavor. A man needs to feel his belly full, all sleepy-eyed after dinner, like a 'gator sittin' on the bank in the sun. See? Even Poochini don' care so much for dis food." He'd hold out a bite of fish and I swear that little buggy-eyed thing would just sniff it and turn his head away.

"What a man needs is some fine chop-meat, like my Grammaw used to fix," Ferris would say.

Ferris' grandmother was a cook for a good many years. Ferris praised up her bread pudding with rum sauce and her homemade pies all the time, but to him her 'chop meat' was apparently the ultimate in cuisine. It sounded vile - a combination of beef scraps, liver, heart, even some tongue if it were handy, all chopped up fine and seasoned with lots of red and Scotch Bonnet pepper, sauteed in butter. Ferris talked about it with this reverent tone in his voice, but I just couldn't bring myself to try fixing it.

In truth, the longer we were together, the less of an appetite I had. Perhaps it was handling food all day at work, but it seemed that it got harder and harder for me to eat dinner in the evening. Oh, I'd have a piece of fruit, maybe a little salad, or a bite of whatever I'd fixed for Ferris, but I just couldn't eat much. As soon as I'd hear Ferris and the dog puffing up the stairs, steps creaking under the weight, I'd begin feeling a trifle ill.

Mind you, I didn't let that prevent me from cooking for him. Ferris did love his food In fact, his love of food, and that little dog, were his only weaknesses. In all our years together, I don't believe Ferris was ever unfaithful. Oh, I heard gossip - one always does, especially with a man as attractive as Ferris was when I met him - but I discounted all that. Mother used to say that idle gossip was the Devil's work. All I know is that Ferris was always home in time for dinner. He'd sit across the table from me, smacking his lips over his dinner and setting aside little special bits for Poochini, and when he got all done, he'd push back his chair and say, "Lily, that was simply fine."

Ferris was my life, you know - Ferris and Poochini, and my job at Broussards. Eventually Ferris began to have spells of indigestion after dinner. Oh, he brushed it off, said it was nothing, but the sweat would break out on his head, and his face would get beet red. Of course, he wouldn't see a doctor - said we couldn't afford one, which was pretty much true. I'd started sleeping on the couch, mostly, I told him, because he snored, but the truth is, there just wasn't room in the bed anymore. Besides, he insisted that Poochini sleep in the bed, too, the dog snorted and snuffled till I thought I'd go out of my mind. Ferris had quit taking him out so much, because the little beggar was getting too fat to climb the stairs.

It seemed as though I was always tired. The couch wasn't all that comfortable, and being a waitress isn't the same adventure at forty that it is when you're in your twenties. I still had my figure, thank goodness, but there were lines in my face that would certainly prevent me from auditioning for anything but a character part. I suppose we all wonder where the years have gone, although Ferris never seemed to think about it.

That Friday night, I got off early. Ferris had gone down to Du Monde for coffee. I could hear him puffing all the way at the bottom of the stairs, and by the time he came in the front door, I had the table all set, candles and everything.

"What's this, Cher?" he said when he could get his breath.

"I just thought I'd do something special for you tonight," I said, pulling out his chair and patting it.

"What are we havin'?" he asked, shoving the chair back a bit more so's he could get seated without his belly grazing the table.

"It's a surprise," I told him.

When I set the platter down in front of him, Ferris leaned over and sniffed the steam rising. He looked up at me. "Cher," he said, beginning to smile, "is this what I think it is?"

"Um-hmm," I said, nodding.

"Lawd!" Ferris said, snatching his fork up like a starving man. "You made chop-meat for me, sugar!" He helped himself to two patties and some fried okra, and took a big bite of the meat.

"Mmmmm, mm! This is good, Lily," he said. There was a ring of grease around his lips, and a little fleck of food dropped from his lip to his chin and hung there.

"Is it as good as your grandmother's ?" I asked.

Ferris took another bite. "Well," he said, closing his eyes, rubbing one hand across his greasy chin, "pretty close. Not quite the same, though."

"I hope it's fine enough. It isn't tough, is it?" I asked.

"Well, maybe a little," Ferris said. He fished around on his plate and picked out a morsel from the center of the other patty. "Poochini! Here, Boy!" he yelled, "Here! Lookit what your Mama fixed for us."

"Is the seasoning wrong?" I asked. "I wasn't sure how much to use."

"Well no, I don't think that's quite it," Ferris said. He frowned. "Poochini! Where IS that damn ol' dog?"

I looked right at Ferris. His hair was mostly all silver now, not just the limp lock in front, and there was grease around his soft, pink mouth, some of it smeared on his shirtfront.

"He's in the kitchen," I said calmly.

Ferris kept chewing for a second or two, making that ugly smacking sound with his lips, and then he looked up at me and all of a sudden his eyes went sort of funny.

"Lily?" he said. He looked down at his plate again, then up at me.

He went red, shook his head and started to get up out of his chair, but he must've sucked in a breath, and all that chop meat shut off his windpipe like concrete. He grabbed his throat and started thrashing around, waving his arms and struggling to get onto his feet, and his eyes were wild. I moved out of his way and just stood there watching. Finally, Ferris fell out of the chair onto the floor, just kind of folded up in a heap, his hands clutching his shirtfront, all spotted with food, his face turning slowly blue. I was sorry then, but seeing Ferris lying there like that, I could see how truly grotesque he was, and Mother always told me to take advantage of every opportunity the good Lord gave me. It seemed like this was the first one I'd had in a very long time.

I took off my apron and hung it up neatly on the peg next to the door. I went on into the kitchen and brought Poochini in from the back porch - poor little thing, he's stone deaf and almost blind, but he does like to catch the coolness in the evenings. Then I tided up a bit, made sure my hair was in disarray, smudged my lipstick for effect and took a deep breath or two to prepare for my performance.

"Hello, operator?" I said when she came on the line. "Could you send someone quickly please? I'm afraid there's been a terrible accident."

Printed in the United States
by Baker & Taylor Publisher Services